Read Love Share

Recommended books
for reading groups

January – June 2011

First published in Great Britain as a collection of sample chapters in 2010
by The Orion Publishing Group Limited
Orion House, 5 Upper St Martin's Lane,
London WC2H 9EA

An Hachette UK company

1 3 5 7 9 10 8 6 4 2

A CIP catalogue record for these books
are available from the British Library.

ISBN 978-1-4091-0886-3

Printed and bound in Great Britain by
CPI Mackays, Chatham ME5 8TD

The Orion Publishing Group's policy is to use papers that
are natural, renewable and recyclable products and
made from wood grown in sustainable forests. The logging
and manufacturing processes are expected to conform to
the environmental regulations of the country of origin.

www.orionbooks.co.uk

Contents

Tiger Hills

Sarita Mandanna

1878

Muthavva knew her seventh child was special, had known from the very day of her birth, the day of the herons. It was a clear day in July. With almost two months to go before the baby was due, and the sowing season upon them, Muthavva had put off leaving for her mother's home. She made her laborious way to the fields instead, and was standing ankle deep in the flooded flats when she heard a rustling. She looked up, shading her eyes against the sun and rubbing the small of her back. A flock of herons wheeled overhead. In itself, this was not unusual. There were herons to be seen in every field in Coorg, the flash of their wings startling against bright green paddy. But in all her years, Muthavva had never seen as many as were now slowly descending upon the flats. A hundred birds, maybe more, flying wingtip to wingtip, casting the sun-drenched fields into shadow. The fluttering of their feathers drowned out the croaking of frogs, the cawing of crows, even the incessant racket of crickets.

Muthavva could no longer hear her brother-in-law's

voice carried on the wind as he called out instructions to the labourers hired to help with the sowing, his words muffled by the steady beat of wings. The birds circled slowly, lower and lower, executing a final sharp turn to land by her feet.

Muthavva stood surrounded, still absently massaging her back amongst a sea of silent white. And then, without warning, the herons took wing again. Up they soared on some secret cue, all around her, showering her with the glittering droplets of water that rolled off their wings and the tips of their feet. At that instant, not one moment sooner or later, Muthavva felt a gush of warm liquid on her thighs. Her daughter was here.

The mountains. That is what the dead must notice first, Muthavva had always believed. That very first time, when they rose from the funeral pyres, slipping through ash, borne by the wind high into the clouds. And from there, that first, dizzying, glorious sight of Coorg.

It was a tiny principality, shaped not unlike the knitted bootie of an infant, and tucked into the highest reaches of the Sahyadri mountains that girded the country's coastline to the south. The far side of the mountains was bounded by the ocean, dropping abruptly into the glittering blue of the Arabian Sea. The way down the cliffs was so slippery, so fraught with loose rocks and sharp-edged shingle, that only the most money-hungry traders were foolhardy enough to attempt it. They assembled twice a year at the edge of the bluffs, in time to meet the Arabian ships docked below, with baskets of captured monkeys whose feet they had painted red with betel juice and lime. They would release the monkeys over the cliffs, driving them down towards the sea with a great banging and bashing of drums; as the monkeys jumped terrified from rock to rock, they left behind a map of tiny red footprints for the traders to follow. Even so, each year there were those who fell, men screaming as they spun through the air, finally smashing onto the rocks far below.

Turning inland, the silver flash of the Kaveri river, ribboning the olivine mountains and parcelling Coorg neatly in two like the halves of a coconut. To the north, the undulating hills of bamboo country, softly rounded, dotted with towering arches of bamboo and slender knots of trees. Blackwood and ironwood, dindul and sandalwood, eucalyptus, benteak and rosewood, interspersed with breezy glades where grasses shimmered in the sun. The Scotland of India. That is what the many white folk in Coorg called it, this part of the land that reminded them so much of Europe. They had set about civilising the central town of Mercara, rechristening its streets Tenth Mile, Queens Way and Mincing Lane. They clustered their estates about the town – coffee plantations sprung from Ceylonese beans that had rapidly taken root in this virgin soil. Their planter bungalows lay in a series of rough circles around the town. Low slung, red roofed and diamond paned, replete with verandahs, croquet lawns and racquet courts.

In stark contrast, the Shola forests of the South. Wild, untrammelled tracts of pipal, cinchona, ebony, toon and poon, crowding in on themselves, adorned with club moss and lush, unscented orchids. Tangles of thorned underbrush erupted between their trunks, vast, laboriously spun cobwebs bridging the exposed corrugation of their roots.

Here and there, scattered almost evenly between the north and the south, the local villages. A velvet patchwork of jungle soil, moist, fertile and dark as the night sky where the forest had been hacked away. Peridot swathes of paddy flats lining the wetlands by the streams. The sprawling, golden-thatched homes of the Coorgs, each with its designated wetlands and grazing pastures and the telltale wisps of smoke that rose from their hearths into the trees.

Finally the forest, at the base of the mountains. The thickly knitted toe of the bootie, forming a protective cover over the tip of Coorg that jutted out towards Mysore. This was dense jungle, simmering with a dangerous, compelling beauty, marked only by the faintest of trails. Only the Coorgs knew the jungle trails well, them and the charcoal-skinned Poleya tribals who served them.

The trails had always been jealously guarded, especially in the old days when Coorg lay under siege. The sultans of Mysore had tried for generations to bring this stubbornly independent principality under their dominion. The internecine warfare, the abductions, the forced circumcisions and mass executions had only served to unite the Nayaks, patriarchs of the eight most prominent families in Coorg. They had banded together, bidding the clans under their jurisdiction to stand shoulder to shoulder against Mysore. The Coorgs resisted the sultans, digging in their heels and clinging to their land like the copper-coloured crabs that burrowed in their fields.

When the British and their John Company had finally overthrown Mysore, the Coorgs had rejoiced as one. In the peace treaty that followed, Coorg was ceded to the British. They had taken the measure of this little province, looked appraisingly at its mist-laden hills and salubrious climes so well suited to the planting of coffee. They took note of the Coorgs; tall, fierce hotheads who thought nothing of looking them in the eye and speaking as one man to another. Wisely they had been patient, pushing their agenda with polite, manicured resolve. Eventually, fifty years after they had taken Mysore, the British were formally welcomed into Coorg.

Still, despite these days of peace and the syenite roads that the British had carved, skirting the edges of the forest to connect Coorg with the neighbouring provinces, collective memory ran deep. There was a band of armed and able-bodied Coorgs always stationed at the bend overlooking the entrance to the forest where the road from Mysore met the mouth of the trail. The Nayaks shared responsibility for manning this post, each staffing it with men from the clans under his dominion for five weeks at a stretch except for the three months of the monsoons when the trails were rendered impassable by mudslides and trees felled by lightning.

Today, the lookout post was quiet. Men lay snoring in the rough bamboo and burlap machan while Nachimanda Thimmaya kept watch. The afternoon wind picked up, gusting through the branches overhead and scattering dried leaves through the machan. Thimmaya shivered, drawing his tunic closer about him. If only he had picked the white cowrie shell this year, curse his luck. When Pallada Nayak, the village headman, had announced the date of the cowrie picking, Thimmaya had gone especially to the Iguthappa temple, offering its all powerful deity, Iguthappa Swami, a whole two rupees, money he could scarcely afford. He had sacrificed a fowl to the ancestors and yet another to the veera, the ghosts of the valiant. Leaving nothing to chance, Thimmaya had even propitiated the wood spirits with a hefty bundle of pork and rice left in the forest. The day of the picking, when the priest had extended his closed fists towards him, Thimmaya had sent up yet another fervent prayer to Iguthappa Swami. But no, he had pointed at a fist and the priest had opened his palm only to reveal a black cowrie; Thimmaya had been selected once more, three years running, to man the post.

This year was especially hard. It was sowing season and

every available pair of hands would be needed in the fields. Muthavva should be in her mother's home, not bending over the paddy, not when her belly swelled round and full with another child. It had been a difficult pregnancy, the dribbles of blood in the early weeks, the pain in her back as her stomach grew. His brother Bopu had offered to take his place at the lookout post, but Thimmaya had refused. Bopu had his own family to feed, and besides Pallada Nayak would not have approved. He sighed. If the price for cardamom fell again this year in Malabar, the family would have to tighten their belts.

He was sitting there, lost in his thoughts, when he started. Someone was running through the jungle calling for him. 'Ayy. Who is it?' he shouted, grabbing his matchlock and peering through the branches.

The runner came into view and Thimmaya recognised him with a pang of alarm. It was one of Pallada Nayak's cattle hands. 'What happened?' he asked tersely, jumping down from the machan.

'The child . . .' gasped the Poleya, wiping the sweat from his face. 'The child is coming.'

Thimmaya's face tightened. The baby was not due for many weeks, wasn't that what Muthavva had said? Why had the pains started so early?

The men crowded round him as he laced his sandals and tucked his dagger into his cummerbund, slapping his shoulder and telling him not to worry. He barely heard them, all his energy focused on reaching his wife as soon as he could. He loped off along the trail towards the Pallada village, the Poleya struggling to match his pace. 'Please, Iguthappa Swami,' he prayed, over and over. 'Please.'

He reached the village just before nightfall, and went first to the Pallada house to pay his respects. The evening lanterns were being lit, casting the Nayak in silhouette as he strode up and down the verandah. 'Ah, Thimmaya, have you come?' he said, pleased, as Thimmaya bent to touch his feet. 'It is good, it is good,' he said, 'now go to your wife.' Thimmaya nodded, unable to speak. 'There is no cause for worry,' the Nayak reassured him. 'All is well.'

Thimmaya nodded again, his chest still tight with fore-boding. He touched the Nayak's feet, then hurried towards his own home, yet a good six furlongs away. It was dark by the time he got there, the lamps had been lit, the dogs fed and let loose for the night. They rushed barking towards him as he stopped at the aimada, the ancestor temple in the courtyard. 'Ancestors of the Nachimanda clan,' he prayed, passing his palms back and forth over the flickering lamps. 'I will sacrifice a fowl to you, please let my woman be well.'

And then his nephews and his son were running out to meet him, and his mother, laughing, her arms extended. 'Uyyi! You have come, monae.'

'Muthavva?'

'She is fine, they are both fine, monae. Come in and see

your pearl of a daughter.'

They brought hot water from the fireplace for him to wash his hands and feet and then he headed for the bedroom where Muthavva lay flushed and spent upon their cot. His mother put the baby in his arms. He gazed down at his wriggling daughter and the knot in his chest came finally undone, dissolving into an emotion so strong he had to blink to stop the tears.

Muthavva never told him about the herons that had heralded the baby's birth. The labour had started so quickly, the pains had been so insistent that her brother-in-law had hoisted her onto his back and run all the way home from the fields. The baby had been in such a hurry to be born that the midwife had barely been summoned before she thrust her way into the world. As the women bustled about, looking for the brass gong to announce the birth of a girl child, and the servants were sent to distribute puffed rice and bananas in the village, Muthavva made up her mind. She had birthed six babies before this child. Six healthy, squalling boys, of which only the oldest, Chengappa, had survived infancy. She touched her finger to the tip of the baby's pert, perfectly formed nose. This daughter, she knew in her heart, was special. Why cloud her birth with talk of omens or portents? No, she decided, she would tell nobody about the birds.

She did, however, once. After the ritual forty days of cleansing were over, when Muthavva untied the cloths bound tight about her abdomen, arose from the birthing bed, and was deemed able to perform her household duties once more, the family took the baby to the village temple to have her horoscope drawn. The old priest reached for his manuscript of tattered pipal leaves wrapped in orange silk and passed down through generations from father to son. The child would have marriage, he predicted, and progeny. Money was in her fate too. But . . . and here he fell silent. Muthavva and Thimmaya looked anxiously at one another. 'What is it, ayya? What do you see?' Thimmaya's mother asked, anxiously clutching the baby closer until she squirmed in protest.

'Nothing . . . it is nothing . . . and yet . . .' The priest fell silent once again and consulted his leaves. He looked up at the worried faces around him, as if debating what to say. 'It is nothing,' he said finally, even as he fished about in a dilapidated wooden box. 'Here.' He pulled out an amulet. 'This will protect her.' The amulet had a powerful mantra inscribed upon it, he advised, it would protect her from the evil eye. Best she wear it at all times. Shushing their concerns, he smeared vermilion on their foreheads and tied the amulet around the baby's arm with black thread.

They touched the feet of the priest and prostrated in front of the idol. They had made their way outside, blinking in the sudden sunlight when, exclaiming that her earring was missing and that it must have fallen off during the reading, Muthavva hurried back inside.

'Ayya?' she called softly, her eyes taking a minute to adjust to the cool darkness of the sanctum sanctorum. The priest was clearing away the debris from their pooja, and he looked up, mildly irritated.

'Yes, child, what is it now?'

She told him about the birds she had seen that day, the unnerving precision of their manoeuvres, as if they had come to herald the baby's birth. What did it mean? What had he seen in the leaves? Was there something he had not told them, some awful fate that awaited her daughter?

The old man sighed. Who could say what they meant, the birds? It was said that when a king cobra happened upon a sleeping man and, instead of sinking its fangs into his flesh, fanned its hood instead, to shelter him from the sun, then that man would someday be king. The herons . . . maybe they foretold something, maybe they did not. Who could read the mind of God?

When Thimmaya went to see Pallada Nayak the next day on his way back to the outpost, the Nayak generously excused him from the remainder of his lookout duty. It was only fair to Muthavva, he said, and besides, it was sowing season, and Thimmaya had another mouth to feed. The Nayak would send his youngest son in Thimmaya's place.

The paddy that year was so bountiful that Thimmaya was able to buy two milch cows with the gold it fetched him; the cardamom prices were the highest they had been in six years. The family sacrificed a cockerel to the ancestors for blessing them with a daughter who brought with her such good fortune. They named her Devamma, after Thimmaya's great-grandmother, but called her Devi, their very own Goddess.

Why I wrote . . .
Tiger Hills

In my homeland of Coorg it was customary to bury the umbilical cord of a newborn. Past the jungle topsoil, past tree root and shale, deep into the earth. It served as a talisman, so that no matter how far one went, no matter the passage of time, this beacon always pointed the way back home. Perhaps inevitably then, when I began to write *Tiger Hills* six years ago, Coorg was the setting that naturally unfurled in my mind. I recalled childhood memories of my grandfather telling us stories around an oil lamp; the great-grandmother, widowed young, who roamed her fields, a dagger tucked into her blouse. These stories and others sunk for generations into these hills.

While Coorg forms the highly personalised canvas of *Tiger Hills*, I also wanted to write a story that was almost classical in scope – a big narrative, and characters who struggle with universal questions. What do we do when thrust into circumstances not of our choosing? When do we stand firm, and when is it best to resign ourselves to a change in direction and move forward the best we can? *Tiger Hills* explores this nexus between fortitude and acceptance, the choices we make in the aftermath of happenstance.

Determined to forge a life for herself within the parameters decided for her, the main character Devi builds a barrier around her heart. To such an extent, however, that she becomes wedded to a version of happiness too rooted in the past to ever become real. At the core of *Tiger Hills* is a love story, but there are other stories too, forming its undercurrent. A missionary, searching. An orphan, single-minded in his devotion. A boy, marked both by the mother who leaves him and the legend of a father barely remembered. A woman who defies expectations to mark out a new path for herself. Different interpretations of love – obsessive, possessive, selfish, unrequited, filial. The suffering we invite upon those we hold dear. Finally, redemption. *Tiger Hills* is an exploration of our all too human need to come full circle, for reconciliation; and the idea that often, it lies well within our grasp.

Sarita Mandanna

The Prestige

Christopher Priest

I t began on a train, heading north through England, although I was soon to discover that the story had really begun more than a hundred years earlier.

I had no sense of any of this at the time: I was on company time, following up a report of an incident at a religious sect. On my lap lay the bulky envelope I had received from my father that morning, still unopened, because when Dad phoned to tell me about it my mind had been elsewhere. A bedroom door slamming, my girlfriend in the middle of walking out on me. 'Yes, Dad,' I had said, as Zelda stormed past with a boxful of my compact discs. 'Drop it in the mail, and I'll have a look.'

After I read the morning's edition of the *Chronicle*, and bought a sandwich and a cup of instant coffee from the refreshment trolley, I opened Dad's envelope. A large-format paperback book slipped out, with a note loose inside and a used envelope folded in half.

The note said, 'Dear Andy, Here is the book I told you about. I think it was sent by the same woman who rang me. She asked me if I knew where you were. I'm enclosing the envelope the book arrived in. The postmark is a bit blurred, but maybe you can make it out. Your mother would love to know when you are coming to stay with us again. How about next weekend? With love, Dad.'

At last I remembered some of my father's phone call. He told me the book had arrived, and that the woman who had sent it appeared to be some kind of distant relative, because she had been talking about my family. I should have paid more attention to him.

Here, though, was the book. It was called *Secret Methods of Magic*, and the author was one Alfred Borden. To all appearances it was one of those instructional books of card tricks, sleight of hand, illusions involving silk scarves, and so on. At first glance, most of what interested me about it was that although it was a recently published paperback, the text itself appeared to be a facsimile of a much older edition: the typography, the illustrations, the chapter headings and the laboured writing style all suggested this.

I couldn't see why I should be interested in such a book. Only the author's name was familiar: Borden was the name I had been born with, although when I was adopted my name was changed to that of my adoptive parents. My name now, my full and legal name, is Andrew Westley, and although I have always known that I was adopted I grew up thinking of Duncan and Jillian Westley as Dad and Mum, loved them as parents, and behaved as their son.

All this is still true. I feel nothing for my natural parents. I'm not curious about them or why they put me up for adoption, and have no wish ever to trace them now that I am an adult. All that is in my distant past, and they have always felt irrelevant to me.

There is, though, one matter concerning my past that borders on the obsessive.

I am certain, or to be accurate almost certain, that I was born one of a pair of identical twins, and that my brother and I were separated at the time of adoption. I have no idea why this was done, nor where my brother might be now, but I have always assumed that he was adopted at the same time as me. I only started to suspect his existence when I was entering my teens. By chance I came across a passage in a book, an adventure story, that described the way in which many pairs of twins are linked by an inexplicable, apparently psychic contact. Even when separated by hundreds of miles or living in different countries, such twins will share feelings of pain, surprise, happiness, depression, one twin sending to the other, and vice versa. Reading this was one of those moments in life when suddenly a lot of things become clear.

All my life, as long as I can remember, I have had the feeling that someone else is sharing my life. As a child, I thought little of it and assumed everyone else had the same feelings. As I grew older, and I realised none of my friends was going through the same thing, it became a mystery.

Reading the book therefore came as a great relief as it seemed to explain everything. I had a twin somewhere.

The feeling of rapport is in some ways vague, a sense of being cared for, even watched over, but in others it is much more specific. The general feeling is of a constant background, while more direct 'messages' come only occasionally. These are acute and precise, even though the actual communication is invariably non-verbal.

Once or twice when I have been drunk, for example, I have felt my brother's consternation growing in me, a fear that I might come to some harm. On one of these occasions, when I was leaving a party late at night and was about to drive myself home, the flash of concern that reached me was so powerful I felt myself sobering up! I tried describing this at the time to the friends I was with, but they joked it away. Even so I drove home inexplicably sober that night. It must be a psychic mechanism of some kind, which we use without understanding it. No one to my knowledge has ever satisfactorily explained it, even though it is common and well documented between twins.

There is in my case, however, an extra mystery.

Not only have I never been able to trace my brother, as far as official records are concerned I never had a brother of any kind, let alone a twin. I do have intermittent memories of my life before adoption, although I was only three when that happened, and I can't remember having a brother at all. Dad and Mum knew nothing about it; they have told me that when they adopted me there was no suggestion of my having a brother.

As an adoptee you have certain legal rights. The most important of these is protection from your natural parents: they cannot contact you by any legal means. Another right is that when you reach adulthood you are able to ask about some of the circumstances surrounding your adoption. You can find out the names of your natural parents, for instance, and the address of the court where the adoption was made, and therefore where relevant records can be examined.

I followed all this up soon after my eighteenth birthday, anxious to find out what I could about my background. The adoption agency referred me to Ealing County Court where the papers were kept, and here I discovered that I had been put up for adoption by my father, whose name was Clive Alexander Borden. My mother's name was Diana Ruth Borden (née Ellington), but she had died soon after I was born. I assumed that the adoption happened because of her death, but in fact I was not adopted for more than two years after she died, during which period my father brought me up by himself. My own original name was Nicholas Julius Borden. There was nothing about any other child, adopted or otherwise.

I later checked birth records at St Catherine's House in London, but these confirmed I was the Bordens' only child.

Even so, my psychic contacts with my twin remained through all this, and have continued ever since.

———————————

The book had been published in the USA by Dover Publications, and was a handsome, well-made paperback. The cover painting depicted a dinner-jacketed stage magician pointing his hands expressively towards a wooden cabinet, from which a young lady was emerging. She was wearing a dazzling smile and a costume which for the period was probably considered saucy.

Under the author's name was printed: 'Edited and annotated by Lord Colderdale.'

At the bottom of the cover, in bold white lettering, was the blurb: 'The Famous Oath-Protected Book of Secrets'.

There was a longer and more descriptive blurb on the back cover:

'Originally printed in London in 1905, by the specialist publishers Goodwin & Andrewson, this book was sold only to professional magicians who were prepared to swear an oath of secrecy about its contents. First edition copies are now exceedingly rare, and virtually impossible for general readers to obtain.

'Made publicly available for the first time, this new

edition is completely unabridged and contains all the original illustrations, as well as the notes and supplementary text provided by Britain's Earl of Colderdale, a noted contemporary *amateur* of magic.

'The author is Alfred Borden, inventor of the legendary illusion *The New Transported Man*. Borden, whose stage name was 'Le Professeur de Magie', was in the first decade of this century the leading stage illusionist. Encouraged in his early years by John Henry Anderson, and as a protégé of Nevil Maskelyne's, Borden was a contemporary of Houdini, David Devant, Chung Ling Soo and Buatier de Kolta. He was based in London, England, but frequently toured the United States and Europe.

'While not strictly speaking an instruction manual, this book with its broad understanding of magical methods will give both laymen and professionals startling insights into the mind of one of the greatest magicians who ever lived.'

It was amusing to discover that one of my ancestors had been a magician, but I had no special interest in the subject. I happen to find some kinds of conjuring tedious; card tricks, especially, but many others too. The illusions you sometimes see on television are impressive, but I have never felt curious about how the effects are in fact achieved. I remember someone once saying that the trouble with magic was that the more a magician protects his secrets, the more banal they turn out to be.

Alfred Borden's book contained a long section on card

tricks, and another described tricks with cigarettes and coins. Explanatory drawings and instructions accompanied each one. At the back of the book was a chapter about stage illusions, with many illustrations of cabinets with hidden compartments, boxes with false bottoms, tables with lifting devices concealed behind curtains, and other apparatus. I glanced through some of these pages.

The first half of the book was not illustrated, but consisted of a long account of the author's life and outlook on magic. It began with the following words:

'I write in the year 1901.

'My name, my real name, is Alfred Borden. The story of my life is the story of the secrets by which I have lived my life. They are described in this narrative for the first and last time; this is the only copy.

'I was born in 1856 on the eighth day of the month of May, in the seaside town of Hastings. I was a healthy, vigorous child. My father was a tradesman of that borough, a master wheelwright and cooper. Our house—'

I briefly imagined the writer of this book settling down to begin his memoir. For no exact reason I visualised him as a tall, dark-haired man, stern-faced and bearded, slightly hunched, wearing narrow reading glasses, working in a pool of light thrown by a solitary lamp placed next to his elbow. I imagined the rest of the household in a deferential silence, leaving the master in peace while he wrote. The reality was no doubt different, but stereotypes of our forebears are difficult to throw off.

I wondered what relation Alfred Borden was to me. If the line of descent was direct, in other words if he wasn't a cousin or an uncle, then he would be my great-or great-great-grandfather. If he was born in 1856, he would have been in his middle forties when he wrote the book; it seemed likely he was therefore not my father's father, but of an earlier generation.

The Introduction was written in much the same style as the main text, with several long explanations about how the book came into being. The book appeared to be based on Borden's private notebook, not intended for publication.

Colderdale had considerably expanded and clarified the narrative, and added the descriptions of most of the tricks. There was no extra biographical information about Borden, but presumably I would find some if I read the whole book.

I couldn't see how the book was going to tell me anything about my brother. He remained my only interest in my natural family.

At this point my mobile phone beeped. It was Sonja, the secretary of my editor, Len Wickham. I suspected at once that Len had got her to call me, to make sure I was on the train.

'Andy, there's been a change of plan about the car,' she said. 'Eric Lambert had to take it in for a repair to the brakes, so it's in a garage.'

She gave me the address. It was the availability of this car in Sheffield, a high-mileage Ford renowned for frequent breakdowns, that prevented me from driving up in my own car. Len wouldn't authorise the expenses if a company car was on hand.

'Did Uncle say anything else?' I said.

'Such as?'

'This story's still on?'

'Yes.'

'Has anything else come in from the agencies?'

'We've had a faxed confirmation from the State Penitentiary in California. Franklin is still a prisoner.'

'All right.'

We hung up. While I was still holding the phone I keyed in my parents' number, and spoke to my father. I told him I was on my way to Sheffield, would be driving from there into the Peak District and if it was OK with them (of course it would be) I could come and stay the night. My father sounded pleased. He and Jillian still lived in Wilmslow, Cheshire, and now I was working in London my trips to see them were infrequent.

I told him I had received the book.

'Have you any idea why it was sent to you?' he said.

'Not the faintest.'

'Are you going to read it?'

'It's not my sort of thing. I've already looked through it. Maybe I'll have another look later.'

'Andy, I noticed it was written by someone called Borden.'

'Yes. Did she say anything about that?'

'No. I don't think so.'

After we had hung up I put the book in my case and stared through the train window at the passing countryside. The sky was grey, and rain was streaking the glass. I tried to think about the incident I was being sent to investigate. I worked for the *Chronicle*, specifically as a general features writer, a label which was grander than the reality. The true state of affairs was that Dad was himself a newspaperman, and had formerly worked for the Manchester *Evening Post*, a sister paper to the *Chronicle*. It was a matter of pride to him that I had obtained the job, even though I have always suspected him of pulling strings for me. I am not a fluent journalist, and have not done well in the training programme I have been taking. One of my serious long-term worries is that one day I am going to have to explain to my father why I have quit what he considers to be a prestigious job on the greatest British newspaper.

In the meantime, I struggle unwillingly on. Covering the incident I was travelling to was partly the consequence of another story I had filed several months earlier, about a group of UFO enthusiasts. Since then Len Wickham, my supervising editor, had assigned me to any story that involved witches' covens, levitation, spontaneous combustion, crop circles, and other fringe subjects. I had already discovered that in most cases, once you went into these things properly, there was not much to say about them, and remarkably few of the stories I filed were ever printed. Even so, Wickham continued to send me to cover them.

There was an extra twist this time. With some relish, Wickham informed me that someone from the sect had phoned to ask if the Chronicle was planning to cover the story, and if so had asked for me in person. They had seen some of my earlier articles, thought I showed the right degree of honest scepticism, and could therefore be relied on for a forthright article. In spite of this, or perhaps because of it, it seemed likely to prove yet another dud.

A Californian religious sect called the Rapturous Church of Christ Jesus had established a community in a large country house in a Derbyshire village. One of the women members had died of natural causes a few days earlier. Her GP was present, as was her daughter. As she lay paralysed, on the point of death, a man had entered the room. He stood beside the bed and made soothing gestures with his hands. The woman died soon after, and the man immediately left the room without speaking to the other two. He was not seen afterwards. However, he had been recognised by the woman's daughter, and by two members of the sect who had come into the room while he was there, as the founder of the sect. This was Father Patrick Franklin, and the sect had grown up around him because of his claimed ability to bilocate.

The incident was newsworthy for two reasons. It was the first of Franklin's bilocations to have been witnessed by non-members of the sect, one of whom happened to be a professional woman with a local reputation. And the other reason was that Franklin's whereabouts on the day in question could be firmly established: he was known to be an inmate of the California State Penitentiary, and as Sonja had just confirmed to me on the phone he was still there.

The writing of . . .
The Prestige

How do ideas for novels develop? The genesis of *The Prestige* is a good example. One day I came across a description of the life and work of a nineteenth century stage magician called Ching Ling Foo. Ching, a real Chinese, was one of the first Oriental magicians to work in the West. By using a traditional Mandarin costume and by habitually wearing an impassive expression, Ching conveyed an unmistakable aura of Oriental mystery, menace and amazing magical powers. He was a conventional magician using conventional techniques, but he made quite an impression.

There were in fact two major Chinese illusionists in this period. Ching Ling Foo was so successful that an imitator called Chung Ling Soo emerged. Chung (not Ching) is probably most famous for the way he died: one night at a theatre in London he was performing the trick where the magician attempts to catch a bullet in his teeth. That night it went disastrously wrong. He was the twelfth magician to die while performing this dangerous illusion, and according to magical folklore the trick has rarely been performed since. Magicians are superstitious – no one wants to be number thirteen.

Chung Ling Soo, incidentally, was not Chinese at all. The confusingly similar name (deliberately chosen, of course) was a *nom de théâtre* for an American illusionist called William Ellsworth Robinson, who was one of several Western magicians who donned Oriental disguise.

Chung and Ching were enemies: each claimed to be able to perform the other's illusions, and derived much publicity from this.

While reading about Ching Ling Foo (the real one) I came across a description of the famous illusion he performed as the climax of his act. It was simple in appearance, but maddeningly impossible to explain. As this trick is described in the early part of *The Prestige* I'll leave you to find out not only what he performed but (unusually, because *The Prestige* does not give away many secrets) how he did it.

The secret of Ching's trick was a revelation to me. Not the technique itself, because that is a slight matter, but the way in which it forced him to maintain the illusion throughout his normal life. He was concealing the secret twenty-four hours a day.

Years later, seeking a fictional story that would metaphorically describe the art of writing fiction, I remembered the techniques a conjuror uses to misdirect his audience. Misdirection is at the heart of magic, as it is in many novels. Without drawing too much attention to what he is doing, a magician places images and ideas before the audience, and allows them to make their own assumptions about what is going to happen. Some novelists do the same.

An example is the moment when a magician produces a brand-new deck of playing cards, still sealed inside their cellophane wrapper. He opens the deck, tosses aside the protective seals, fans the cards to display them, then performs a trick. Most people in the audience will make the assumption that by opening the deck in front of them the magician is proving two matters. Firstly, that the cards were sealed up until that moment. Therefore, secondly, he couldn't have interfered with them in any way.

This is exactly what the magician wants the audience to think, because the opposite is almost certainly the case. At no point does the conjuror deliberately mislead the audience, or lie to them: he uses misdirection, allowing the audience to make its own assumptions, and the trick is performed before anyone can think it through.

Getting interested in magic, I remembered the way Ching Ling Foo had allowed a secret to dominate his life, and how that in turn had created curiosity in other magicians and in one particular rival an almost obsessive desire to better him, or expose him.

The two magicians in my novel, Borden and Angier, are similar rivals, but I have spared my readers the confusion of similar names. However, in the same kind of way as Chung and Ching they are both harbouring secrets that enable them to perform, and it's not long before they are plotting to destroy each other, little realizing the obsessive nature of a well-kept secret.

So there you have the way *The Prestige* came into being. In describing it, I have, so to speak, opened what seems to be a brand-new deck of cards, have tossed aside the cellophane wrapper, and now I am fanning the cards before you. The simple appearance of the trick that is about to be performed can be understood by everyone. But as you now realize, by writing this preface I have already begun to misdirect you. Watch carefully, and try not to blink . . .

Christopher Priest

PS: I have written a book about the genesis of *The Prestige*, the way the film came into being, and the differences that exist between the novel and the film. The book is called *The Magic*, and it can be obtained through my website: www.christopher-priest.co.uk

The Frozen Heart

Almudena Grandes

The women weren't wearing tights. Their fat, fleshy knees bulged over the elastic of their socks, peeking out from under the hem of their dresses, which were not really dresses but shapeless, collarless smocks made of some lightweight fabric I could not name. I looked at them, planted like squat trees in the unkempt cemetery, wearing no stockings, no boots, and with no other coat than the coarse woollen jackets they kept closed by folding their arms across their chests.

The men weren't wearing overcoats either, but their jackets – made of a darker shade of the same coarse wool – were buttoned up to hide the fact that they had their hands in their pockets. Like the women, they all looked identical – shirts buttoned to the throat, heavy stubble, hair close cropped. Some wore caps, others were bare headed, but, like the women, they adopted the same stance: legs apart, heads held high, feet planted firmly in the ground like stout trees, ancient and strong, impervious to cold or catastrophe.

My father, like them, had had no time for people who were sensitive to the cold. I remembered that as I stood with the icy wind from the sierras slashing at my face – 'a bit of a breeze', he would have called it. In early March the sun can be deceitful, pretending to be riper, warmer, on one of those late winter mornings when the sky seems like a photograph of itself, the blue so intense it looks as though a child had coloured it in with a crayon – a perfect sky, clear, deep, translucent; in the distance, the mountains' peaks still capped with snow, a few pale clouds ravelling slowly, their unhurried progress completing this perfect illusion of spring. 'A glorious day', my father would have said, but I was cold as the icy wind whipped at my face and the damp seeped through the soles of my boots, my woollen socks, through the delicate barrier of skin. 'You should have been in Russia, or Poland, now that was cold', my father would say when as kids we grumbled about the cold on mornings like this. 'You should have been in Russia, or Poland, now that was cold'. I remembered his words as I stared at these men, these hardy men who did not feel the cold, men he had once resembled. 'You should have been in Russia, or Poland', and the voice of my mother saying, 'Julio, don't say things like that to the children . . .'

'Are you all right, Álvaro?'

I heard my wife's voice, felt the pressure of her fingers, her hand searching for mine in my coat pocket. Mai turned to me, her eyes wide, her smile uncertain; the expression of someone intelligent enough to know that, in the face of death, there is no possible consolation. The tip of her nose glowed pink and the dark hair that usually tumbled over her shoulders lashed at her face.

'Yes,' I said after a moment. 'Yes, I'm fine.'

I squeezed her fingers and then she left me to my thoughts.

There may be no consolation in the face of death, but it would have pleased my father to be buried on a morning like this, so similar to the mornings when he would bundle us all into the car and drive to Torrelodones for lunch. 'A glorious day, just look at that sky, and the Sierra! You can see all the way to Navacerrada. The air is so fresh it'd bring a dead man back to life . . .' Mamá never enjoyed these trips, though she had spent her summers in Torrelodones as a child and it was where she had met her future husband. I didn't enjoy them either, but we all loved him – his strength, his enthusiasm, his joy – and so we smiled and sang *'ahora que vamos despacio vamos a contar mentiras, Átra-la-ra!, vamos a contar mentiras'*, all the way to Torrelodones. It's a curious town: from a distance, it looks like a housing estate, but as you draw nearer it seems to be nothing more than a train station and a scatter of buildings. 'You know why it's called Torrelodones?' Of course we knew, it was named after the little fortress that perched like a toy castle on top of the hill, the Torre de los Lodones, yet every time we came he would explain it to us again. 'The fortress is an ancient tower built by the Lodones, they were a tribe, a bit like the Visigoths . . .' My father always claimed he didn't like the town, but he loved taking us there, to show us the hills and the mountains and the meadows where as a boy he had tended sheep with his father; he loved to wander the streets, stopping to chat with everyone, and afterwards telling us the same stories: 'That's Anselmo – his grandfather was my grandfather's cousin. That woman over there is Amada and the woman with her is Encarnita, they've been friends since they were little girls. That man over there, his name's Paco, he had a vicious temper, but my friends and I used to steal apples from his orchard . . .'

At the slightest sound Paco would rush out of his house waving his rifle, though he never actually shot at the boys who were stealing his cherries, his figs. Anselmo was much older than my father; by rights he should have been long dead, yet here he was at my father's funeral, and beside him Encarnita. Beneath the wizened mask of old age, I could still see the plump, friendly faces that had smiled into my childish eyes. It had been years – more than twenty years – since that last 'glorious Sunday morning' when my father had taken us to Torrelodones for lunch. I hadn't been back since and the sight of all these people moved me. Time had been cruel to some of them, gentler to others, but they had all washed up on the shore of an old age that was very different to my father's. At some other time, some other place, some other funeral, I probably wouldn't have recognised them in the dark mass of huddled bodies, but that morning I stared at each of them in turn, at their powerful bodies, their solid legs, their natural, almost haughty, formality, their shoulders aged but not bowed, their dark, tawny skin, weathered by the mountain sun which burns but does not tan. Their cheeks were etched with long wrinkles, deep as scars. No delicate web of crow's feet round their eyes, but deep, hard lines, as though time had carved their faces with a chisel thicker than the fine blade it had used on my father.

Julio Carrión González might have been born in a little house in Torrelodones, but he died in a hospital in Madrid, his skin ashen, his eldest daughter – an intensive care doctor – in attendance, and with every tube and monitor and machine available. Long ago, before I was conceived, his life had taken a different path from the lives of the men and women he had known as a boy, the people who had outlived him, who had come to his funeral as if from another time, another world, from a country that no longer existed. Life had changed in Torrelodones too. I knew that if they had time, if they knew someone with a phone, a car, these people would also die surrounded by tubes and monitors and machines. I knew that the fact that they still left the house without an overcoat, a purse or tights said little about their bank balance, which had been steadily growing over the years thanks to the influx of people from Madrid prepared to pay any price for a plot of land barely big enough to graze a dozen sheep on. I knew all this, yet looking across the grave at their weather-beaten faces, the stocky frames, the threadbare corduroy trousers, the cigarette butts clenched defiantly between the lips of some, what I saw was the abject poverty of the past. In the fat, bare knees of these women with nothing to keep out the cold but a coarse woollen jacket, I saw a harsher, crueller Spain.

We stood on the opposite side of the grave. His family, the well-dressed product of his prosperity, his widow, his children, his grandchildren, some of his colleagues, the widows of former colleagues, a few friends from the city I lived in, from the world I knew and understood. There weren't many of us. Mamá had asked us not to tell people. 'I mean, Torrelodones, it's hardly Madrid,' she said, 'people might not want to come all that way . . .' We realised that she wanted only those closest to her at the funeral, and we had respected her wishes. I hadn't told my sisters-in-law, nor my mother's brothers, I hadn't even told Fernando Cisneros, my best friend since university. There weren't many of us, but we weren't expecting anyone else.

I hate funerals, everyone in the family knows that. I hate the gravediggers, their offhand manner, the predictable, hypocritical expression of condolence they put on when their eyes accidentally meet those of the bereaved. I hate the sound of the shovels, the grating of the coffin against the sides of the grave, the quiet whisper of the ropes; I hate the ritual of throwing handfuls of earth and single roses on to the coffin and the insincere, portentous homily. I hate the whole macabre ceremony, which inevitably turns out to be so brief, so banal, so unimaginably *bearable*. That's why I was standing with Mai off to one side, almost out of earshot of the droning voice of Father Aizpuru, the priest Mamá had invited from Madrid. The man who, she claimed, had kept her children on the straight and narrow, the priest my older brothers still treated with the same infantile reverence he had cultivated when he refereed football matches in the schoolyard. I'd never liked him. In my last year in primary school, he was my tutor, and he used to make us exercise in the playground stripped to the waist on the coldest days of winter.

'Are you men or are you girls?' Another image of Spain. He would stand there, his cassock buttoned up while I shivered like a freshly sheared lamb in the fine cold drizzle of sleet. 'What are you – men or girls?' I never joined in the enthusiastic chorus shouting 'Men!' because there was only one thought running through my head: 'You bastard, Aizpuru, you fucking bastard'. Naive as I was, I tried to get my own back at the age of sixteen, as I sat stony faced through Friday mass, refusing to pray, to sing, to kneel, 'fuck you, Aizpuru, it's your fault that I lost my faith'. Until finally he phoned my mother, called her into school after class and had a long chat with her. He told her to keep an eye on me. 'Álvarito isn't like his brothers,' he said, 'he's sensitive, headstrong, he's weaker. Oh, he's a good lad, a first-rate student, responsible and clever too – maybe too clever for a boy his age. That's what worries me. Boys like that develop unhealthy friendships, that's why I think it might be best for you to keep an eye on him, keep him busy.' That night my mother sat on the edge of my bed, ran her fingers through my hair, and without looking at me, said: 'Álvaro, *hijo*, you do like girls, don't you?''Of course, Mamá, I like girls a lot.' She heaved a sigh, kissed me and left the room. She never asked me about my sexual orientation again and never said a word to my father. I graduated top of my class, with the same refrain still ringing in my head, 'you fucking bastard, Aizpuru, you fucking bastard', never suspecting that years later I would realise that he was right, not me.

'Álvaro, *hijo*, I know you didn't want to wear a suit and tie today, but please, I'm begging you, at least be pleasant to Father Aizpuru . . .' This was the one thing my mother had asked of me that morning, so I'd made sure I was the first to shake his hand so that my somewhat frosty greeting would be forgotten in the exaggerated fuss my brothers Rafa and Julio would make of him, hugging the fat old man, who ruffled their hair, kissed them on both cheeks, all of them blubbering and crying. The Marist brotherhood of brotherly love, 'I have two mothers, one here on earth, the other in heaven'. A clever piece of bullshit. I said as much to Mai and received a swift kick for my pains. Clearly, my mother here on earth had had a word with my wife.

Father Aizpuru was right, I wasn't like my brothers, but

I was a good lad, always. I'd never been a problem child, never caused trouble the way they had. In the innumerate, unscientific world I'd grown up in, my better-than-average flair for mental arithmetic had bestowed on me a mythical intelligence that even I did not believe I possessed. Yes, I'm a theoretical physicist, and that's a job title that causes a few raised eyebrows when people first hear it. Until they discover what it means in reality – a professor's salary and no prospect of becoming what they would consider to be rich and important. That's when they realise the truth – that I'm just a normal guy. At least I was until that morning when my one phobia – my morbid aversion to funerals – propelled my mind from the profound, universal grief of the survivor into a curious state of heightened awareness. It probably had something to do with the pill Angélica had given me at breakfast. 'You haven't cried, Álvaro,' she said. 'Here, take this, it'll help.' She was right, I hadn't cried – I rarely cry, almost never. I didn't ask my sister what the pill was – and maybe my detachment was simply down to me refusing to deal with my grief – but as I stood there feeling strangely alert I turned my gaze from the fat, fleshy knees of the women from Torrelodones to the faces of my own family.

There they stood, and suddenly it was as though I didn't know them. Father Aizpuru was still blethering on, my mother was staring out towards the horizon, the sea-blue eyes of a young woman set in an old woman's face, her skin so translucent, so fine, it seemed as though it might split from all the wrinkling, folding and fanning out. My mother's character was not in her wrinkles, however, but in her eyes, which seemed so gentle yet could be so harsh, their shrewdness masked by the innocence of their colour; when she laughed they were beautiful but when she was angry, they flared with a purer, bluer light. My mother was still a handsome woman, but when she was young Angélica Otero Fernández had been a beauty, a fantasy – blonde, pale, exotic. 'Your family must be from somewhere in Soria,' my father used to say to her. 'You have Iberian blood in you, they have blond hair and pale eyes . . .' 'Julio,' my mother would say, 'you know perfectly well that my father is from Lugo in Galicia, and my mother is from Madrid.' 'That may be, but somewhere in the distant past. Either that or your father had Celtic blood,' he insisted, unable to think of any other reason for the superiority of my mother's genes, which had produced a string of pale, blond, blue-eyed children; a string broken only once, when I was born.

'Gypsy', my brothers used to call me, and my father would hug me and tell them to shut up. 'Don't pay them any attention, Álvaro, you take after me, see?' In time, that fact became increasingly obvious. Father Aizpuru had been right, I wasn't like my brothers, I didn't even look like them. I glanced over at Rafa, the eldest, forty-seven – six years older than me – still blond, although he was now almost bald. He stood next to my mother, stiff and serious, conscious of the solemnity of the occasion. Rafa was a tall man, with broad shoulders in proportion to his height and a pot belly that stuck out from his skinny frame. Julio was three years younger but looked almost like his twin, though age had been kinder to him. Between them came Angélica – now Dr Carrión – who had extraordinary green eyes and who envied me my dark complexion, since she had pale, delicate skin that burned easily. The mysteries of the Otero/Fernández bloodlines had produced better results in the female of the species than the male. My brothers were not particularly handsome, but both my sisters were beautiful and Clara, the youngest, was stunning. She too was blonde, but her eyes were the colour of honey. Then there was me. In the street, at school, in the park, I looked completely unremarkable, but at home I was totally out of place, as though I were from another planet. Four years after Julio was born and five years before Clara, along I came, with my black hair, dark eyes and dark skin, narrow shoulders, hairy legs, big hands, and a flat stomach – the lost Carrión, shorter than my brothers, barely as tall as my sisters, different.

On the day of my father's funeral, I hadn't yet realised how painful that difference would turn out to be. Father Aizpuru went on murmuring and the wind went on blowing. 'You should have been in Russia, or Poland . . .' my father would have said, because it was cold, I felt cold, in spite of my scarf, my gloves, my boots, I felt cold even though I had my hands in my pockets and my coat buttoned up, even though I wasn't blond and fair skinned, even though I wasn't like my brothers. They felt the cold too, but they hid it well, they stood to attention, hands clasped over their coats, exactly as my father must have stood at the last funeral he attended. He would have worn that same expression – so different from the patient resignation I saw in the eyes of Anselmo and Encarnita, who were in no hurry, who no longer expected to be surprised, bowed only by time, drawing strength from their terrible weariness so that they could look reluctantly on the lives of others. This, I thought, was what my father had lost when his life diverged from theirs. He had been luckier than they had because although money does not make for a happy life, curiosity does; because although city life is dangerous, it is never boring; because if power can corrupt, it can also be wielded with restraint. My father had had a great deal of power and a great deal of money in his life and had died without ever being reduced to the vegetable, the mineral state of these men, these women he had known as a child, and who, at the moment of his final farewell, had come to claim him as one of them.

He was not one of them. He had not been one of them for a long time. That was why I was so moved to see them, huddled together on the far side of the grave, not daring to mingle with us, Julio Carrión's widow and his children. If I had not stared at them, had not accepted the quiet challenge of their bare knees, the coarse woollen jackets, perhaps I might not have noticed what happened next. But I was still staring at them, wondering whether they had noticed that I didn't look like my brothers, when Father Aizpuru stopped talking, and, turning to look at me, spoke the terrible words: 'If the family would like to come forward.'

Until that moment, I had not been aware of the silence; then I heard the sound of a car in the distance and was relieved as its dull roar masked the dirty clang of the shovels digging into the earth, the harsh grating that seemed to rebuke me, the cowardly son, Father Aizpuru's unruly pupil. 'If the family would like to come forward,' he had said, but I didn't move. Mai glanced at me, squeezed my hand. I shook my head and she went over to join the others. Next come the ropes, I thought, the wheezing and panting of the gravediggers, the brutal indignity of the coffin banging against the walls of the grave, but I heard none of this as the profane, reassuring sound of the engine drew closer, then suddenly stopped just as the shovels finished their work.

There were not many of us, but we weren't expecting anyone else. And yet someone had turned up now, at precisely the wrong moment.

Almudena Grandes

An author insight

There is a reason why Almudena Grandes's novels go straight to number one and sell over 300,000 copies in her native Spain – in fact there are several! First of all, she is a virtuoso storyteller and knows just how to keep her readers expectations balanced on a knife-edge. Her books are always full of surprises and revelations, twists and turns, and *The Frozen Heart* has even more than most because it deals with the secrets of a generation who grew up during the Spanish Civil War. Because this was a war driven by differing ideologies and not specifically national identity, it divided families and friends, neighbours and lovers; brothers found themselves fighting against their siblings or their fathers, cousins against cousins and as the situation escalated, many people were betrayed by those they had previously trusted, even loved. In this book, perhaps the worst betrayal emanates from a character who is driven not by political beliefs, but by a fundamental selfishness that causes him to swap sides several times, chameleon-like, in order to pursue his own aims – stealing a fortune from those he pretends to help and turning his back on his own mother and sister.

That is another reason why Almudena's books have such appeal – her characters take on such a life of their own, they have intense emotional resonance and depth. The author loves to explore the fact that real behaviour, the way humans act, is made up of many shades of grey and in her books, the difference between 'good' and 'bad' is never clear cut. Is an act wrong, if ultimately it results in retribution for the sins of a previous generation? How far should a person go in wanting to protect their family? What is the balance between personal happiness and being true to your beliefs? There is a tremendous warmth and deep humanity in the way Almudena Grandes portrays her characters – she gets to the very heart of what motivates us and how we decide what is important in life.

When I first started reading this book, I thought I knew a reasonable amount about the Spanish Civil War. As I read on, I realised I knew next to nothing. But I never felt as if I was reading a historical tome or academic analysis – and that is another reason why Almudena Grandes's books are so popular. The books are page-turners, driven by a compelling plot and strong characterisation, yet through the interwoven stories you learn about an incredibly fascinating and complex moment in history, from the Blue

Brigades in Russia to the Communist exiles living in Paris, for this was a war that had ramifications well beyond the borders of Spain. In the end, the novel has that most gratifying effect – it holds you in its grasp right until the last page, but you also finish the novel feeling you have learned something.

Kirsty Dunseath

Publishing director of fiction at Weidenfeld and Nicolson

The Singapore Grip

J.G. Farrell

The Blacketts, on the whole, had reason to be satisfied with the calm and increasingly prosperous life they were leading in Singapore in 1937. Only once or twice in the two decades following the Great War had anything occurred to disturb their peace of mind and even then nothing that could be considered particularly serious. True, their elder daughter, Joan, had shown signs of becoming involved with unsuitable young men . . . but that is the sort of thing that any family with growing children has to expect.

Although his wife, Sylvia, became greatly agitated, Walter himself was inclined to take it calmly at first. Joan, who had recently returned from a finishing school in Switzerland, had found it hard to settle down in Singapore, separated from the friends she had made in Europe. She was rebellious, contemptuous of the provincial manners of the Straits, as one naturally would be, Walter supposed, after being at such a school (the school, incidentally, had been her mother's idea). Given time it was something that she would get over.

Joan's involvement with the first of these young men,

a penniless flight-lieutenant whom she had met nobody knew where, was an act of rebellion probably. Even Joan had not tried very hard to pretend that he was anything but impossible. Besides, she knew well enough what her parents, who took a dim view of the Services, thought of even those generals and air vice-marshals whom duty had called to Singapore, let us not speak of flight-lieutenants. Walter had not set eyes on the person in question because Joan had had the good sense not to try to bring him home. He had waited calmly for her to see reason, explaining with a touch of exasperation to his wife that her tears and her fretting were a waste of energy which she could use to greater profit in some other direction, because Joan would presently come to her senses with or without the aid of her mother's tears. In due course, it had taken a little longer than he had expected, Walter's confidence had been justified. Joan had disposed of the flight-lieutenant as surreptitiously as she had found him. Tranquillity had returned to the Blackett household for a while.

Presently, however, it transpired that Mrs Blackett, testing the material of one of Joan's cotton frocks between her finger and thumb, felt an unexpected crinkle of paper. Ah, what was this? Something left by the laundry? Mrs Blackett had happened to grasp the light material of her daughter's frock just where there was a pocket. Joan, who was in the frock at the time, blushed and said that it was nothing in particular, just a piece of paper of no importance.

'In that case,' replied Mrs Blackett, 'we had better throw it away immediately, because it does not do to let our clothes bulge out in an ugly fashion by carrying unnecessary things in our pockets.' Quick as a flash her fingers darted into the pocket and retrieved the offending piece of paper (as she had suspected! a love-letter!) before Joan had time to retreat. The ensuing scene, the shrieking and hysterics and stamping of feet, even reached Walter who was upstairs in his dressing-room at the time, brooding on business matters. He gave the storm a little time to blow over but it showed no sign of doing so and at last he was obliged to come downstairs, afraid that they might burst blood-vessels in their passion. His appearance quelled mother and daughter instantly: they gazed at him glassily, breasts still heaving, faces tear-stained. He promptly sent Joan to her room and, when she had gone, reminded his wife that she was under instructions to take these matters calmly.

'The fact is, my dear, that these emotional scenes do no good at all. Quite the reverse. I should like to know how much you have found out about this young man as a result of all this shouting and screaming? My bet is . . . nothing.'

It was true. Mrs Blackett hung her head. Joan had declared that she would rather be dead than reveal the least thing about him, where she had met him, where he worked, even what his name was. 'His name appears to be "Barry",' said Walter with a sigh, perusing the letter, 'and I can even tell you where he works, since he has written on his firm's notepaper. As to where she met him, that is of no importance whatsoever. So all you have succeeded in doing is putting Joan's back up. In future kindly consult me before you say anything to Joan about her boyfriends. I shall now go and have a word with the young lady.'

Walter climbed the stairs thoughtfully. The marriage of his daughters was a matter to which he had not yet given a great deal of attention. And yet it was undoubtedly a matter of great importance, not only to Joan, as it would be, in due course, to little Kate, his younger daughter, but potentially to the business as well. After all, if you are a wealthy man you cannot have your daughter marrying the first adventurer who comes along. To allow such a match is to invite disaster. The fact was that Joan would do far better for herself and for Blackett and Webb Limited if she agreed to marry someone whose position in the Colony matched her own.

There were, as it happened, two or three young men in Singapore with whom a satisfactory alliance of this sort could have been made and who, given Joan's attractions, would have asked for nothing better. But when, on her return from her finishing school, such a union had been suggested to her, Joan had been indignant. She found the idea distasteful and old-fashioned. She would marry whom she pleased. Naturally the elder Blacketts in turn had been indignant. Walter had demanded to know why he had paid good money to such a school if not to drill some sense of reality into her. But Joan had been stubborn and Walter had quickly reached the conclusion that patience was the best policy. They would wait and see, tactfully fending off unsuitable young men in the meantime. Despite the scene which had just taken place Walter remained confident that Joan was too sensible a girl to remain permanently attached to someone whom her parents considered unsuitable.

Walter, climbing the stairs, had considered rebuking his daughter and ordering her not to communicate with this young man again. Instead he decided to continue banking on her good sense and merely said: 'Joan, dear, I've no objection to you flirting with young men provided you are sensible about it and don't do anything you might regret later. What I do object to is the fact that you have upset your mother. In future please be more discreet and hide your love-letters in some safe place.' Joan, who had been expecting another row, gazed at him in astonishment as he handed her back the letter which had caused all the commotion.

Was Walter taking a great risk with his daughter's future by responding so mildly? Mrs Blackett was inclined to think that he was. Walter, however, reassured her. He was on friendly terms with the chairman of the firm on whose notepaper the young man wrote his love-letters and saw him frequently at the Club. He was confident that if the worst came to the worst and Joan persisted in taking an interest in him, it would require only a nod and

a wink to have the fellow moved away from Singapore
to a convenient distance (back to England if necessary).
As it turned out, this intervention was not necessary: at
a certain age nothing can be more stifling to enthusiasm
than the permission or approval of your parents. 'Barry',
(whoever he was), lovelorn, was allowed to continue his
residence in Singapore.

Mrs Blackett now decided that the best way to prevent
Joan from carrying on with unsuitable young men was to
surround her with suitable ones. True, there was a serious
shortage of the latter in Singapore but she would draw up
a list and see what could be done . . . Joan's trouble was
that she never met anyone of the right sort. Mrs Blackett
would put an end to that by inviting one or two young
men chosen by herself to tea once a week. Joan would be
asked to act as hostess and Walter would be there, too, to
keep an eye on things. What did Walter think of it? Was it
not a good idea?

Walter was dubious. He doubted whether Joan would
take an interest in any young chap of whom her mother
approved. He was even more dubious when he saw the list
that she had drawn up. But in the end he agreed, partly
because he saw no reason why his wife should not have her
own way for once, partly because he had a secret weakness.
This weakness, which was so mild and agreeable it might
almost be considered a virtue, was for holding forth, as
a man with some experience of life, to younger men just

starting out.

So it would happen, once these weekly tea-parties were inaugurated, that while Joan sat tight-lipped and rebellious, her green eyes as hard as pebbles, Walter would grow animated and have a jolly good time. Mrs Blackett meanwhile, would dart glances from her husband to her daughter to the young guest trying to estimate what impression each was making on the other. As a matter of fact, the young man usually sat there looking faintly alarmed as Walter harangued him: after all, this was Blackett of Blackett and Webb, an important man in the Straits, and his parents had told him to be careful not to put his foot in it and to behave himself properly for once.

For a number of years now it had been Walter's agreeable habit to take his visitors by the arm and escort them along the row of paintings that hung in his drawing-room. So it happened that the young man intended for Joan, although on the whole he felt safer sitting down and less likely to knock something over, would reluctantly allow himself to be plucked out of his chair while Joan continued to sit mutinously silent beside the tea-pot, ignoring her mother's whispered entreaties that she should say something to her guest, and even accompany the two men across the room.

Some of the paintings which Walter was showing the young man were primitive in style, painted perhaps by a native artist or by a gifted ship's officer in his spare time: here was a three-masted vessel being loaded with spices or sugar, a line of native porters with bundles on their heads marching in uncertain perspective along a rickety quay surrounded by jungle. In the next painting, by a more sophisticated hand, the ship had arrived in Liverpool and was being unloaded again, and after that would come three or four paintings of the port of Rangoon and Walter would exclaim: 'Look! They're loading rice. Still all sailing ships, of course, and Rangoon's just a sleepy little village. But you wait!'

In the early days, he would explain, while the youth at his side gazed at him uneasily, white rice would not survive the long passage round the Cape and so it was shipped as what was known as 'cargo rice', that is, one-fifth unhusked paddy and four-fifths roughly cleaned in handmills. Throughout the East, to India mainly, it was shipped simply as paddy ('The blighters cleaned it themselves.'). Now Walter, unreeling history at a prodigious speed, would guide his guest (well, Joan's guest) to a later picture of Rangoon. 'You see how it's grown in the meantime. And see how steam has taken the place of sail in the harbour (though some ships still have both, of course). And these great buildings with chimneys, d'you know what they are? Steam rice-mills!'

For now it was possible, with the opening of the Suez Canal in 1870, to ship cleaned rice to Europe, thereby cutting out the fine-millers who used to clean the 'cargo rice' in London.

'Ruined 'em,' Walter would remark with a frown. 'They weren't quick enough. A businessman must keep his wits about him.' And if the young man happened to be starting out on a business career himself, as he probably was, Walter might pause to lecture him on how you must always be ready to move with the times, never taking anything for granted.

'Go and join them!' hissed Mrs Blackett to her daughter in a penetrating whisper. 'You're being impolite to your guest.'

'But Mother, I've told you a thousand times . . .' And it was true . . . she had.

The last picture of Rangoon had been painted after the turn of the century and showed how the thriving rice trade had caused it to spread and grow into a great modern city, now only surpassed as an Eastern port by Calcutta and Bombay. Walter would draw his dismayed captive closer and after a moment's examination of the teeming wharves on the Rangoon River he would put his finger on a fine warehouse and say. 'Our first! The first to belong to Blackett and Webb . . . or rather, to Webb and Company as the firm was then called. We still have another exactly similar here in Singapore on the river. Well now, you see how a bit of trade can make a place grow?' And with an air of satisfaction he would lead the suitable young man on to yet more paintings of Calcutta, Penang, Malacca, and of Singapore itself, in various stages of development.

'You see how we made these little villages grow in just a few years. That's what a bit of tin and rubber have done for Singapore!'

There was still another painting to be seen, and one that was more important than all the others, but by now Mrs Blackett was growing impatient and calling Walter and his audience back for another cup of tea. These tea-parties, she was beginning to think, were not having the desired effect. A disturbing thought occurred to her and she eyed her daughter suspiciously. Could it be that the reason for Joan's lack of interest in her guest was that she was already carrying on in secret with yet another unsuitable young man?

J. G. Farrell and
The Singapore Grip

The last two years have seen a renaissance for one of Britain's most remarkable authors. Four decades after it was first published, J.G. Farrell's novel *Troubles* was awarded the Lost Man Booker Prize for 1970. Two years earlier, in 2008, *The Siege of Krishnapur* was short-listed for the Best of Booker Prize. The sudden upsurge of enthusiasm for this author was intense: the media hailed him as a genius whose praises were unsung for too long and *Troubles* won more than double the votes cast for any other book on the Booker list. Farrell's writing has that rare quality of being both serious and wonderfully humorous at the same time that inspires absolute loyalty in fans.

James Gordon Farrell was born in Liverpool in 1935 but spent much of his time in Ireland. His life was cut short in that country when he was just forty-four after he was swept out to sea in County Cork whilst fishing. Many of the recent articles on Farrell have mused on just what the literary world lost through that tragedy. At the time, the shock of losing such a promising writer in his prime was such that the Provisional IRA, suicide and MI5 plots were bandied about. Now it's accepted that Farrell was knocked off a narrow ledge and paralysed by hypothermia and shock almost instantly. Fortunately for us, he was able to complete a hugely ambitious literary project – his Empire trilogy – before his death.

The Singapore Grip is the final novel in that trilogy and gives a glimpse into the brutal way the elegant lives of the British in Singapore were chewed up by the Second World War. As in both *Troubles* and *The Siege of Krishnapur* Farrell wryly illustrates the fragility of civilisation and the extent to which our nation was so unable to contemplate the idea of its own vulnerability that it was literally staring down the barrel of a Japanese rifle before it reacted. The theme of tumultuous change echoes throughout all three books and in *The Singapore Grip* Farrell introduces us to the Blackett family, whose prosperous world of cocktails and tennis parties is trembling on the brink of extinction as the Japanese army approaches.

Farrell was fascinated by the last gasp of the British Empire and all it meant, commenting 'It seemed to me that the really interesting thing that's happened during my lifetime is the decline of the British Empire'. He felt that as half-Irish and half-English he was able 'to look at the same thing from both sides – from that of the colonist and the colonised'. This satirical detachment and Farrell's ability to put the reader in every character's shoes, no matter how absurd they might be, lends *The Singapore Grip* a richness and emotional pull that few authors can claim.

The Empire trilogy is often categorised as 'historical fiction' but this description is hardly adequate. J.G. Farrell is one of the wittiest and most sardonic writers of his generation and the Empire trilogy is both morally ambitious and a compelling portrait of changing times. The novels also stand alone as pure, joyous entertainment. Farrell had a knack of creating the most sympathetic and believable of characters and placing them in atrocious circumstances. Walter Blackett, as he stands amidst his crumbling world, is as touching a character as any you'll meet in fiction.

Gail Paten

Paperback editor at Orion Books

The Drowning People
Richard Mason

AN EXTRACT

My wife of more than fifty years shot herself yesterday afternoon.

At least that is what the police assume, and I am playing the part of grieving widower with enthusiasm and success. Life with Sarah has schooled me in self-deception, which I find – as she did – to be an excellent training in the deceiving of others.

Of course I know she did nothing of the kind. My wife was far too sane, far too rooted in the present to think of harming herself. In my opinion she never gave a thought to what she had done. She was incapable of guilt.

It was I who killed her.

And my reasons were not those you might expect. We were not unhappily married. Sarah was, until yesterday, an excellent and loving wife. She was conscientious, in some respects, to her core. It's funny, that – how completely contrasting standards can coexist in a person without seeming to trouble them. My wife was, at least outwardly, never anything but dutiful, correct. 'She gave of herself tirelessly in the service of this island and its people' – that's what the chaplain will say of her when the time comes, and he will be right.

Sarah had many virtues, chief amongst which was an unflinching sense of duty made graceful by serene execution. That is what she will be remembered for. And her serenity was not only for herself: she had a way of making the lives of those around her serene also. It was serenity on her terms, of course, but I would have welcomed it on anybody's terms when I married her, and that has held true over fifty-seven years.

If you knew me, you wouldn't think me at all the murdering type. Indeed, I don't consider myself a violent man and I don't suppose that my having killed Sarah will change that. I have learned my faults over eighty-two years on this earth, and violence – physical, at least – is not amongst them. I killed my wife because justice demanded it, and by killing her I have seen a sort of justice done.

Or have I? Doubts trouble me. My obsession with sin and punishment, laid to rest so imperfectly so long ago, is returning. I find myself wondering what right I had to judge Sarah, and how much more harshly I will be judged for having judged her.

It might not have come to this. I might never have known. But Sarah's inexorable sense of wifely duty exposed her. She was organizing a surprise party for my birthday, not that anything remains a secret for long on this island. I've known something was afoot for a month or more. And I was touched. But I'm particular about parties. I don't like the tenants invited, and I don't like some of Sarah's more fawningly agreeable friends. So it was only natural that I should want to consult a guest list so that by hinting at least I could have made my wishes known.

I chose yesterday to search her desk because my wife was out, supervising the extension to the ticket office. And quite by chance I found the drawer she has kept it in all these years.

Even now, with her dead and nearly buried, the arrogance of it chills me.

———————————

I am in the little sitting room (in days gone by a dressing room) that connects my bedroom to Sarah's. It is the warmest room in this icy house because it is the smallest.

Very little of the world's clutter bothers me here. This is precisely as I wish it. I don't approve of technology – all those little gadgets, each one more fragile than the last. Constantly breaking. I refuse to have a mobile telephone. With both doors closed and a fire blazing and the radiators on under its pointed Gothic windows, this room is like the world as it once was – before everyone communicated endlessly. It is almost cosy.

There is no desk in here, only a sofa, two chairs, and

a small table covered with books. Their inscriptions have long since faded; their givers are dead. They have sat on that table for more than forty years, I should think: a bible, calf-bound, from my mother; my grandfather's *Fowler's*; Donne's love poetry, an old edition of Ella's borrowed long ago. There is a music stand in the corner too, a graduation gift from my parents. From where I sit I can see my initials engraved on its base:

For J. H. F. June 1934.

June 1934; almost sixty years ago. That stand was mine before I ever knew her.

It is important to me that I should have explained myself to myself by the time everyone arrives. The coroner's inquest is set for tomorrow. Then there'll be the funeral and the interment, and the house will be full of people. From this evening there'll be no peace for weeks. If ever I am to put the events of my life in some sort of order I must begin the sifting now.

It is curious, my lack of compunction; not complete, perhaps, but almost. Now that Sarah is gone and I know the truth, I feel very little. Hardly any outright regret. Just a curious, empty, almost eerie, calm: a numbness that shows me, perhaps, quite how much I have learned from her. It strikes me that in some ways I should be glad, though I am not; that the absence of gladness is a striking one, for years ago this knowledge would have freed me. It would have given me what some call a new lease of life. I might have gone back. So it is odd that I should feel nothing now, or at most next to nothing.

The events of those weeks long ago, in which the seeds of it all were sown, have a playlike quality. They belong to a lost time before the war. I know the plot and can empathize with the characters; but the young man of twenty-two who plays such a central part is a stranger to me. He bears little relation (beyond a slight, decreasing, physical similarity) to the image that confronts me as I pass the looking-glass by the fireplace, as I stare at the books, at the music stand, at the waves and the gun-grey sky.

My life seems to have slowed. The present takes up so much time. I see myself as I was at twenty-two. Very young, certain physical gangliness characterizing my movements (I was tall, with long legs). My mouth is thin-lipped, my eyes a pale brown. All are set in a regular oval face with small ears and a slightly pointed chin. Hardly handsome.

I suppose my family life and upbringing must go some way to explaining why my adult life has turned out as it has. My father was a man of deliberate gesture and unshakeable self-belief, a quality I don't think he succeeded in passing on to me. What he did give me is stubbornness. It has sustained me when all else has failed, when arrogance and self-belief have deserted me.

What did my parents want for me? What were they like? It is so difficult to know. We were not rich. We knew rich people, and I suppose that my parents, like any parents, hoped that their son would go far in the world. In *their* world, I should say. They did not look outwards. They never ventured beyond the narrow range of their own ambition. They read *The Times* and voted Conservative and held unchanging and predictable views on the events of the day. Because they were kind they insisted on planning my future on their own terms, with all the tenacity of challenged sincerity.

My own private plan of becoming a concert violinist, flatly and sullenly expressed in my last year at Oxford, met with no favour. My late adolescence was marked by the slow build-up of family tension, its explosive release and subsequent subsidence over long days of icy politeness.

It is ironic that I should end my life in a house like this one, with a titled wife whose family history is as weighty as any to which her parents-in-law could ever have aspired. It is ironic too that, having made so much of following my own lights, I have succeeded ultimately in achieving only what my parents wished for me all along. My musical career died gradually as my marriage progressed. Sarah could not hope to fuel it as Ella had done, nor did she try to; and my reserves of emotion have dwindled unavoidably over time. My talent lay in translating private passion into public performance. As the private passion stopped flowing, dried, and finally turned to a dust so fine that the slightest wind scattered it to nothingness, there was no longer anything to be translated. Technically I remained pre-eminent, for I have always been diligent; but I stopped playing when I could hope for nothing more than mechanical brilliance.

My education was unremarkable. I was clever enough to go to Oxford, which was a great relief to my parents; and until the age of nineteen I made a creditable enough return on their investment in my private education. But at university I was encouraged, by those I knew and the books I read, to cultivate a certain detachment from home life and its aspirations for me, a detachment which made me critical during term-time and superior in the holidays. It was then I turned with real determination to my secret love, the violin. And it was then, comparatively late but in time enough, that I had the leisure and the teaching to discover that I might be really good: good enough to matter. Good enough, certainly, to use my music as the basis for my first serious confrontation with my parents, which raged the whole of the summer of 1934 and centred around my stubborn insistence that I was destined to be a musician.

But I digress. I remember what I looked like at twenty-two; I see the boy's half-smile and his rosy cheeks and the hair tumbling over his forehead into his eyes. But I don't know him at all. I have no empathy with his tastes and only a little with his enthusiasms, surprisingly few of which have remained.

I struggle to remember the people with whom he filled his life, the friendships he made. He was curiously intense, for he was a young man of extremes, inclined to manic sociability and profound gloom by turns. Of course, a few stand distinct from the tableau. People like Camilla Boardman, the girl my mother always hoped I would marry: pretty, confident and well connected. More substantial than she liked to seem. But I was insular at twenty-two. Indiscriminately friendly, I shared myself intimately with great discrimination. I still do. Perhaps I had little to share. Life was as it was and I accepted it on its own terms, much in the way I would later accept my marriage to Sarah: with a dogged determination I would not admit to myself.

Unthinking, unseeing, unknowing, I drifted through life until I met Ella. It was she who threw me into the sea of life. And she did it quite unthinkingly, little caring how much good or how much harm she might do. It was in her nature, that wild abandonment, that driving need for experience and explanation. It was she who made me swim, she who pushed me from the safety of the shallows. It was she with whom I floundered, out of my depth. It is to her, and to my memories of her, that I must turn now in seeking to explain what I have done.

In memory she is a small, slight girl, my age, with tousled blonde hair and green eyes that sparkle back at me complicitly, even now. She is in a London park, Hyde Park.

It is an early morning in mid-June. Birds sing. Keepers in green overalls are setting up deckchairs. The air is sweet with the scent of newly mown grass. I can hear myself panting.

I had been running, up early and out of the house to escape the frost that had settled since my acceptance to the Guildhall. My father had strict views on the desirability of merchant banking. My mother, usually a useful ally, sided with him, saying that no grandchildren of hers would grow up in Hounslow because their father was an impoverished musician. I had begun by reminding them that many musicians make a living. Later more violent things were said. The atmosphere at home had not yet recovered from the latest scene, staged two days previously, and I had no wish for another meal of silent recrimination.

So I went running in the park. I can feel the pulse of the blood beating in my head, see what I wore: a white singlet; school rugby shorts; the socks of my College boat club. I can see what Ella wore, too, because I noticed her long before she saw me. She was sitting on a bench, in a black dress that pulled tight against her slender hips. Her eyes were dazed from wakefulness. A pearl necklace (which I have since, on another's neck, come to know well) was in her closed hand. She was a dramatic figure in the half-light of the early morning. I ran past her twice before she noticed me, each time shortening the route by which I doubled back unseen and passed her again. The third time

I passed, she looked up at me and her eyes focused. She smiled.

I stopped, panting, a little distance from the bench, regretting my last circuit of the carriage track. When I turned to look at her she was still smiling.

'I'm sure I know those socks,' she said. 'They're College socks, aren't they? There are so many kinds of sock in England.'

'They're the socks of my College boat club,' I said with adolescent pride.

Remembering it now, I find it curious to think that the course of my whole life hung on something as inconsequential as my choice of footwear that morning. Ella would not have noticed different socks. Without her remarking on them as she did, I would probably never have known her, because I'd never have found a way of talking to her on my own. In that case I would not be the person I am today; I would not have killed my wife yesterday afternoon; I would not be in this smoky room, trying to keep warm, listening to the waves of the Atlantic crash on the rocks beneath my windows.

I watch myself saunter over to the bench where she is sitting, a question on my lips. Ella remains absolutely motionless, the fine bones of her neck and shoulders showing clearly through her pale skin. She is a little hunched, which contributes to the effect of her fragility. She would look innocent but for the cut of her dress and the stylish parting of her short hair, which a hand pushes back from her eyes occasionally and ineffectually. Getting close, I see that pronounced cheekbones make her face almost gaunt, as do pale blue rings which undercircle her eyes. But the eyes themselves are bright: sharp and green, they move swiftly up and down me.

'Oriel, Oxford, aren't they?' she says.

'How do you know?' I ask, smiling.

There is a pause while the smile on her lips fades and she looks serious once more. Her fingers become conscious of the string of pearls in her left hand, which she puts into a small square bag at her feet with an unconscious gesture of protection.

'I know someone who has them.' 'Who?'

'You wouldn't have known him, unless you're older than you look.'

Since she doesn't seem disposed to say anything further, I question her more closely, telling her that one never knows.

'His name's Charles Stanhope,' she says, uttering a name I do not recognize. I say this and she looks up at me and smiles.

'I'm sorry to have interrupted your run. But I've been sitting out here on this bench for so long I think I'd've stayed here for ever if someone hadn't disturbed me and broken the spell.'

'What spell?'

'The spell of wakeful hours.'

She looks up at me, eyes twinkling. I see her fumble absently in her bag for a cigarette case, watch her light one and follow silver-grey smoke circles upwards to a pale blue sky.

The park is noticeably warmer now. People are trickling in, and as they pass they cannot help but look at us, an odd pair under the trees. I can smell the faint odour of sweet perfume and soap and stale cigarette smoke that surrounds her; hear the click of her lighter flint as she makes a flame; see, as she holds her cigarette, that one of her nails is bitten to the quick.

'Have you been out here all night?'

She nods, with a tightening of pale lips. 'Oh yes. This bench and I are old friends. It's heard more of my secrets than it cares to remember.'

'Has it offered good advice?'

'That's just where benches have the advantage over people. They don't offer advice. They merely sit, listening, reminding you by their immovability that nothing in life is that earth-shattering.' She looks up at me. 'I suppose you think me very melodramatic.'

'Not at all.'

I'm itching to ask her more but am constrained by . . . what? By twenty-two years of being told that it is rude to pry. By a fear she is troubled by love for another, whom I instinctively hate.

'You are very polite,' she says eventually, in a tone that sours the compliment.

I nod, and as I do so her words sound in my ears like an accusation. I feel that something is required of me, but what it is I do not know, and as I am not experienced in talking to pretty women I say nothing.

'I wonder if that is your personality or your education,' she goes on. 'This admirable respect you seem to have for my privacy. In your place I'd be curious to know what prompts a fully grown woman to sit up all night in a lonely park and grow garrulous with the larks.'

'Would you tell me if I did ask?' I say quietly.

'Five minutes ago I might have done.' She closes the clasp of her bag with a click. 'But you've cheered me up too much for confidences. And of course this old bench is still just where it was last night, a fine example to us all.' She smiles and pats the worn wood of its seat. 'I feel better now, and less inclined to bore you with my troubles.'

'They wouldn't bore me at all.'

'I'm glad to know you have *some* human curiosity.'

We both laugh again.

'Could I ask your name, at least?'

I'm braver now that I sense she is about to go.

'You could. A name is the least private thing about a person.'

She gets up and leans over to stub out her cigarette on the ground. I see she isn't wearing any shoes and watch her pick up a black silk pair that have been collecting dew under the bench. There is a pause.

'Well, then, what *is* your name?'

'I'm Ella Harcourt,' she says, standing, and offers me her hand.

I shake it.

'And you are?'

'I'm James Farrell.'

'Well, Mr Farrell . . .'

There is a slight awkwardness between us, born of an intimacy almost attempted and just missed.

'It was a pleasure,' she says at last. 'Enjoy the rest of your run.'

And she turns to go, barefooted, her shoes in one hand. I see the redness on her heels where the pumps have been chafing her. She walks delicately, but purposefully and quickly. She does not look back. I sense that she knows I am watching her. It is a long time before she is gone completely from my view, because the carriage track is straight and almost empty.

I look after her shrinking form, hearing the thud of my pulse once more, aware of tiny sounds usually lost: the scratch of squirrels' claws on bark; an indignant magpie.

Richard Mason

An author insight

It is hard to believe how young Richard Mason was when he wrote his impressive début *The Drowning People*. A precociously gifted eighteen-year-old, he was first in a cohort of youthful Oxbridge-educated authors, including Zadie Smith and Hari Kunzru, whose stellar advances and good looks ensured a media brouhaha that would intimidate the most seasoned veterans on the literary circuit.

Published in 1999, as Mason graduated from Oxford, *The Drowning People* was as memorable for its opening line as the hype that surrounded its acquisition. 'My wife of more than forty-five years shot herself yesterday afternoon,' narrator James Farrell tells us. More Daphne du Maurier than Notting Hill, this was not what anyone expected of the handsome Old Etonian.

Within a page James confesses his wife Sarah did not commit suicide. He murdered her. Over the following 350 pages the ageing narrator reveals why. The plot unfurls with the pain and fear of ancient arthritic hands releasing hold of something treasured. The narrator wanders wraith-like through buried memories of an idyllic youth shattered by passions felt more strongly than they were understood.

At twenty-two James is awkward and idealistic. It is the 1930s and he is fresh from Oxford, a gifted violinist on the verge of a glittering career. A chance encounter with the enigmatic Ella Harcourt leads him to fall in love. But she is not free: she is engaged to the doltish Charles Stanhope and enslaved by the expectations that accompany illustrious families.

She is also deeply flawed, whether by madness or caprice, she reveals herself as manipulative and cruel. Demanding first that James helps her escape, her insistence that he prove his love has terrible and lasting consequences.

Dominant in *The Drowning People* is the theme of innocence and experience and how these inform our understanding of relationships. It is also revealed as a poor excuse for denial. James is wracked by guilt at the recognition of the impact his relationship with Ella had on others, especially the young French musician Eric.

Blood and inheritance are also strong themes in the novel. Cousins Ella and Sarah share an ancestor whose suicide has had repercussions down the generations. Each is haunted by a legacy of mental instability, and it is at this point that Mason's writing is at its most vivid and raw, informed no doubt by the suicide of his sister Kay in 1986, as well as his own experiences.

The author has spoken openly about his own struggles with mental health – following the publication of *The Drowning People* he suffered severe panic attacks and considered abandoning his writing career. His struggles are an indictment of the burden we place upon the precociously gifted.

Mason's experience as an outsider, albeit one well-disguised, is also reflected in *The Drowning People*. His Eton vowels hide South African origins – he was educated in the UK because his parents were being punished for their opposition to the Apartheid regime. Both Ella and James are outsiders. At twenty-two James is in a rush to obscure his bourgeois origins and fit in with a glittering aristo set. Ella has had her cut glass Englishness watered down by an American upbringing, to the disgust of her wider family, and works hard for acceptance.

This theme has recurred in Mason's subsequent fiction, including *The Lighted Rooms*, which fiercely challenges national, historical and personal mythologies in an exploration of both the British legacy in South Africa, and our understanding of dementia and appreciation of the wisdom of the old.

Doppelgängers also feature the novel – and, as with the old German legend, destruction follows when they meet. Ella and Sarah are mirror images – they reflect each other's light and darkness. James's *doppelgänger* is Eric, and though James seeks to contrast his older self with the reckless youth he recalls, for the reader the parallels are a clear reminder that we are all products of our past.

In many ways it is a pity Mason's youthfulness dominated the hype surrounding publication of *The Drowning People*. Such a rich and vividly drawn emotional landscape would be an achievement for any writer, whatever their age. As it is, the book heralded the arrival of an author of considerable talent and compassion.

Danuta Kean

Cultural commentator and publishing analyst.
Her work appears in national newspapers, including the
Financial Times, Independent on Sunday *and* Daily Mail.
She lectures on the MA in Creative Writing
at Brunel University

The Breaking of Eggs
Jim Powell

When I was first ill I wanted to eat nothing. After a couple of days, with womanly concern, Madame Lefèvre appeared in my apartment with a bowl of soup and some bread. She had the key to my apartment, of course, and for all I know had frequently inspected its contents while I was away. Indeed she could have been reletting the rooms for six months of every year. I would not have known. I had no reciprocal knowledge of her apartment; in fact I had never been inside it. But I had always imagined this cauldron of soup simmering on her hob, constantly replenished, never entirely depleted, bubbling away over the decades. I had speculated what would be revealed if this soup was subjected to carbon dating. I suspected it would show trace elements of every year since Madame Lefèvre had acquired the building, whenever that had been.

Now she was knocking at my bedroom door and offering me a real bowl of this imagined soup, a bowl that perhaps contained minute particles of a cabbage harvested at the Liberation, a bowl that offered me the opportunity to eat our shared history. As the days went by and I became stronger, other offerings emerged from across the landing:

omelettes, cheeses, a *fricassée* of chicken. Few words were exchanged, apart from those two significant remarks, but I must admit that a certain pressure built up to commence a conversation, to express something more than polite appreciation for her care. Perhaps that was why she did it. Maybe she was lonely. Maybe I was.

It still took me well into January to summon the nerve and to find the words to say. In the end I think I said: 'Madame Lefèvre, we have known each other for a long time. I think it would be appropriate for you to call me Feliks.'

'Thank you Monsieur Zhukovski, I mean Feliks,' she said. There was a pause while she summoned equal nerve. 'And do please call me Sandrine, if you would care to.'

'Thank you, Sandrine,' I said. And then neither of us knew what to say, so we smiled at each other and no doubt both thought how ridiculous it was not to have said those few words many years before.

Madame Lefèvre was the first to recover from our mutual embarrassment and she did it by plunging into the previously taboo subject of politics.

'Have you heard what's happening in Lithuania?' she demanded.

I had heard. It had been on the radio that morning. Soviet troops were storming Vilnius in an attempt to prevent Lithuanian independence.

'It won't do them any good,' she said. 'It's far too late

for that sort of thing now.'

'I dare say you are right,' I replied. Then, feeling that this sounded like a terminal remark to a conversation that had barely started, I wondered what else I could say. 'For me it is a funny thing to think of Lithuanian independence,' I said. 'I was not brought up to think of Lithuania as an independent country.'

'Really?' she said. 'Well that's communism for you.'

'It was not communism actually, Sandrine. I grew up in Poland before the war, before communism.'

'I always wondered if you might be Polish.'

'Yes I am. By birth anyway. And of course for many centuries Lithuania was part of Poland, as I am sure you know.' Madame Lefèvre did not know. She seemed to have little intrinsic interest in the history of Lithuania. I did not have much myself, as a matter of fact. I think she felt the conversation had strayed from its original starting point, namely her great satisfaction at the collapse of communism.

'I'm surprised at you being a communist, Feliks, especially with you being Polish.'

'Not so much a communist,' I said. 'I have always described myself as a leftist.'

The distinction did not impress Madame Lefèvre. 'Same difference,' she said.

I did not know myself why I insisted on the distinction. I used to tell myself it was to do with accuracy and precision, but of course 'leftist' is a less precise term.

It could describe anyone from a hard-line Marxist to a moderate Social Democrat. So was I trying to conceal something? No, I do not think so. I never hid my opinions from anyone. Perhaps I had an abhorrence of labels, of being put in a box neatly labelled 'communist'. Perhaps it was a simple declaration of independence. As time went by, the qualification came closer to the truth. By 1991, I did not know whether I was any longer a communist or not, and it was ceasing to matter. But I did know I was still very much a leftist.

'When did you leave Poland?' By now it was clear that neither the history of Poland nor the precise ideological distinctions of the left would deter Madame Lefèvre from finding out more about me after 36 years.

'In 1939,' I said. 'My brother and I were sent to stay with an aunt in Switzerland.'

'The war again.'

'I do not think so. I believe it was something else.'

'What else could it have been?'

'Oh, personal things,' I said.

'Were there problems at home?'

Well, really! Not a word for 36 years, and then this sudden inquisition into the most private family matters.

'It was a long time ago,' I said. 'A great deal has changed since then.'

'And a great deal is changing now,' she said, accepting my return of the conversation to less personal matters. 'It must be disappointing for you.' The last remark may have suggested sympathy, but did not convey it.

'Yes, it is disappointing for me,' I said. 'It is not what I hoped would happen. I do not like a lot of the changes that are taking place in eastern Europe. I do not expect they will prove to be changes for the better. I preferred things as they were before, when everything was settled and everyone knew where they were.'

'If I may say so, Feliks, I find it strange that someone who wanted to change everything should find himself regretting change.'

'And if I may say so, Sandrine, I find it strange that someone who wanted to change nothing should find herself welcoming it.'

She had no answer to that. Indeed, there was no answer. It depended on what sort of change one was looking for, if any. It was in fact a long time since I had sought change of any kind, in the world or in my own life. As a young man, in the years after the war, I was fearless for change. I wanted everything to change and believed that it would. But at some point, and I cannot now remember when it was, I came to accept things the way they were, to accept my own life the way it was. After that, I no longer looked for change. An ideological split divided Europe. I accepted that. I worked on one side of the divide, where my heart was or where I thought it was, and the rest of the time I lived behind enemy lines. I accepted that too.

I found myself telling Madame Lefèvre about my travels the previous summer and what I had discovered. I did not know if it interested her. I doubted she had set foot outside France.

Perhaps she had never set foot outside Paris. Certainly, everywhere else was foreign and where I went was communist foreign, or had been, which was worse still.

'How much longer will you do it for?'

'I do not know,' I said. For the previous week, restless in a slowly improving illness, I had thought of little else. I had reached no conclusions.

'Is there someone who could take it over?'

'I do not think so,' I said. 'I mean, the only other person involved is the printer and I do not think he could do it or would want to.'

'Could you sell it?'

'I do not know. Perhaps.' I remembered the approach I had received three months earlier from the American firm. 'Actually, someone did contact me recently about it.'

'What did you say?'

'Nothing. I did not reply. I was not interested.'

'Why not?'

That was an easy question, but I was reluctant to admit to the honest answer. There were of course any number of reasons why the enquiry might have led to nothing, but only one reason why I did not even want to discuss it. In the end, I did give the honest answer.

'It was from an American company.'

'So?'

'Sandrine, it is probably hard for you to understand, but I do not want to sell my *Guide* to the Americans. It goes against everything I have believed my entire life, everything I have done. It would be a complete betrayal.'

Madame Lefèvre shrugged her shoulders. 'Well, I don't know,' she said. 'It's your business. But I can't see what harm it would do to talk to them. Still, if you want to cut your nose off to spite your face, that's up to you.'

'It is important to me.'

'Still?'

'Yes. I do not know how to explain it to you. It is not just a question of what I believe. It is also . . . well, I suppose that for a great deal of my life the Communist Party was my family. And you do not turn your back on family.'

'Perhaps not,' said Madame Lefèvre. 'But sometimes family turns its back on you.' And I still recall the sourness with which she spoke those words.

That concluded our belated foray into the art of conversation. I did not doubt that others would follow assuming I remained in Paris, in that apartment. Would I? I spent the rest of the day thinking about the *Guide* and its future, my future. I still did not want to sell to the Americans, but no one else had expressed an interest. What was I saying? That I refused to sell the *Guide* to a capitalist company? That was tantamount to saying I refused to sell it to anybody. Would it be a better epitaph for the *Guide* if it subsided to nothing, accompanying me sickly through my declining years? I was forced to admit that, actually, it would be rather appropriate, but it was not what I wanted.

Then there was the question of money. It had never been my first priority, nor needed to be, but it could not be ignored. I was not rich. I had some savings, but they were not huge. Pension provisions in France were generous, but they would not enable me to stay in this apartment indefinitely, assuming that I wanted to. There was no one to look after me if I became ill, apart from Madame Lefèvre, and she was a good deal older than I was. Conscience was all very well, but if I did not assume responsibility for my own life, who would? If I were living in a different society, maybe things would be different, but I was not.

Sandrine Lefèvre was right. There was no harm in having the conversation. I hauled myself out of bed and rummaged in my desk for the discarded letter. Eventually I found it. It was from a Mike Martins, who styled himself the European Vice-President of a New York firm called Bergelson & King. I decided that, as soon as I was well enough, I would telephone Mike Martins and see if he was still interested.

Why I wrote . . .

The Breaking of Eggs

First novels are often said to be autobiographies in disguise. This one isn't. In fact, I went to great lengths to create a central character who was as unlike me as possible. Feliks Zhukovski is a lapsed Communist. I am not. He reacts to the fall of the Berlin Wall with a mixture of astonishment and regret. I reacted to it with astonishment and delight. He had a childhood disrupted by war that lacked stability and emotional warmth. Luckily, I suffered from none of those. He is pompous, arrogant and self-deluding. I am . . . no – I think I'd better stop there.

So when I first thought of Feliks as my main character, I wasn't sure it was a good idea. For a start, I didn't like him. Would I want to sit in a bar having a drink with this man, I asked myself? No. So why would anyone else want to read about him? But *The Breaking of Eggs* is about change, regeneration and second chances at a late stage in life – and those themes are no strangers to me. It is also about the restriction of ideological certainty, compared with the warmth and chaos of close human relationships – another subject close to my heart, and close to the times I have lived in. So Feliks and I have things in common.

And he is not dislikeable. It just takes a while to get to know him. He is funny, even though he doesn't always intend to be. He has provocative thoughts. He, and other members of his family, have tragic histories that demand our sympathy. And, by the end of the book, he has even become human. This is the Feliks I would have a drink with. And we would insult each other royally. Perhaps we are more like each other than I thought.

Jim Powell

The Prince of Mist

Carlos Ruiz Zafón

Max would never forget that faraway summer when, almost by chance, he discovered magic. It was 1943 and the winds of war were dragging the world relentlessly towards the abyss. In the middle of June, on Max's thirteenth birthday, his father, an eccentric watchmaker and inventor of dazzling if completely impractical devices, gathered the family in the living room to announce that this would be their last day in the lofty apartment perched high above the oldest part of the city, a place that had been their home ever since he could remember. A deathly silence fell upon the members of the Carver family. They looked at each other, and then at the watchmaker. He had that smile on his face they all knew so well, the one that always meant he had bad news or another of his crazy ideas.

'We are moving,' he announced, 'to a beach house in a small town on the coast. We're getting out of this city and away from the war.'

Max gulped then timidly raised his hand in protest. The other members of the family joined in, but the watchmaker waved away their concerns. He was on a roll now, and he laid out his plan with military precision. There would be no going back on the decision: they were leaving the next morning at dawn. Now they had to pack up their most prized possessions and prepare for the long journey to their new home.

In truth, the family was not entirely surprised by the news. They all suspected that the idea of leaving the city in search of a better place to live had been on Maximilian Carver's mind for some time; everyone, that is, except his son Max. To him, the news felt like a mad steam train hurtling through a china shop. His mind went blank, his mouth sagged and his eyes glazed over. As he stood, transfixed, it occurred to him that his entire world – his friends at school, everyone he hung about with, even the corner shop where he bought his comics – was about to vanish forever.

While the rest of the family went off to pack up their belongings, finally resigned to their fate, Max remained staring at his father. The watchmaker knelt down and placed his hands gently on his son's shoulders. The look on Max's face spoke volumes.

'It might seem like the end of the world to you now, Max, but I promise you'll like the place we're moving to. You'll make new friends, you'll see.'

'Is it because of the war?' asked Max. 'Is that why we have to leave?'

A shadow of sadness fell across his father's eyes. All the drive and conviction of the speech he had made to them earlier was gone, and it occurred to Max that perhaps his father was the one who was most afraid of leaving. If he had pretended to be excited about the move, then it was because it was the best thing for his family. It meant there was no other option.

'It's bad, isn't it?' Max asked.

'Things'll get better. We'll be back. I promise.'

Maximilian Carver hugged his son and smiled mysteriously, then pulled an object out of his jacket pocket and put it in Max's hands. It was a shiny oval that hung from a chain. A pocket watch.

'I made it for you. Happy birthday, Max.'

Max opened the silver watch. The hours on the face were marked out by moons that waxed and waned to the rhythm of time, and the hands were rays of a sun radiating out from the centre of the dial. On the case, engraved in fine script, were the words '*Max's time machine*'.

For a second Max wished his father's latest invention really could stop time. Yet, when he raised his eyes and glanced through the window it already seemed to him as if the light of day was receding and the endless city of spires and domes, of chimneys weaving cobwebs of smoke across the iron skies, had started to fade away.

Years later, as he remembered the scene, his family wandering to and fro with their bags while he sat in a corner clutching the watch his father had given him, Max knew that this was the day he left his childhood behind.

That night Max didn't sleep a wink. While the rest of the family slept he lay awake, dreading the dawn when he would have to say goodbye to the small universe he had built for himself over the years. The hours crept by silently as he lay stretched out on his bed, his eyes lost in the blue shadows that danced on the ceiling, as if he might find in them some oracle that could predict his destiny; in his hand, the watch his father had made for him. The moons glowed in the darkness of the night – perhaps they held the answer to all the questions he had begun to ask himself that afternoon.

Finally day began to break over the horizon in a streak of red light. Max jumped out of bed and went down to the living room. His father was sitting in an armchair, fully dressed, reading a book by the light of an oil lamp. Max was not the only one who had spent a sleepless night. The watchmaker smiled at him and closed his book.

'What are you reading?' asked Max, pointing at the thick volume.

'It's a book about Copernicus. I take it you know who he is?' asked Mr Carver.

'I do go to school, you know,' said Max.

His father sometimes still treated him as if he were a child.

'Well what do you know about him?' his father insisted.

'He discovered that the earth turns around the sun, not the other way round.'

'Not bad. And do you know what that means?'

'Problems,' Max replied.

The watchmaker smiled and handed Max the hefty tome.

'Here, it's yours. Read it.'

Max inspected the mysterious leather-bound volume. It looked as if it was a thousand years old and might house the spirit of some age-old genie trapped in its pages by an ancient curse.

'Well now,' his father said abruptly, 'who's going to wake your sisters?'

Without looking up from the book, Max shook his head to indicate that he was granting his father the honour of dragging his two sisters – Alicia, aged fifteen, and Irina, aged eight – out of their beds.

While Maximilian Carver walked off to give the rest of the family their wake-up call, Max settled into the armchair and began to read. He lost himself in the words and images conjured in his mind and for a while forgot that his family was going anywhere. He found himself flying among stars and planets, but then he looked up and saw his mother standing next to him with tears in her eyes.

'You and your sisters were born in this house,' she murmured.

'We'll be back,' he said, echoing his father's words. 'You'll see.'

His mother smiled at him and kissed him on the forehead.

'As long as you're with me, I don't care where we go,' she said.

His mother had a way of reading his thoughts. Half an hour later, the entire family passed through the front doorway for the last time, heading towards a new life. Summer had begun.

Why I wrote . . .

The Prince of Mist

Authors are often asked why they do what they do. Often by themselves, as they sit wondering why they didn't become corporate lawyers or dentists or arms dealers. Why do we choose this strange profession that would rank right below the vocational do-gooder in a list of the least-likely-to-bring-success occupations in the world? I can't speak for my colleagues, but as far as I am concerned, I write because I really have no other choice. This is what I do. This is what I am.

I am in the business of storytelling. I always have been, always will be. It is what I've been doing since I was a kid. Telling stories, making up tales, bringing life to characters, devising plots, visualizing scenes and staging sequences of events, images, words and sounds that tell a story. All in exchange for a penny, a smile or a tear, and a little of your time and attention.

I write for a living. I've been writing and making stuff

up to make ends meet since I left school. It is my way of surviving, of earning a living and of navigating this world. It is my way of bringing something to the table, contributing what I believe is the best thing I have to offer for others to enjoy.

I have written for young readers, for the movies, for so-called adults; but mostly for people who like to read and to plunge into a good story. I do not write for myself, but for other people. Real people. For you. I believe it was Umberto Eco who said that writers who say they write for themselves and do not care about having an audience are full of shit, and that the only thing you write for yourself is your grocery shopping list. I couldn't agree more.

As I said, I am in the business of storytelling. This is an art, a craft and a business, and I thank the Gods of Literature for that. I believe that when you pick up something I've written and pay for it, both in terms of your money and something much more valuable, your time, you are entitled to get the best I can produce. I believe this is not a hobby, it is a profession. If you're pretentious enough to believe that what you write might be worth other people's time (as I am), you should work hard enough to earn that privilege (as I do). Which brings me back to the question of why I write. Sometimes people ask me what piece of advice I would give to an aspiring author. I'd tell them that you should only become a writer if the possibility of not becoming one would kill you. Otherwise, you'd be better off doing something else. I became a writer, a teller of tales, because otherwise I would have died, or worse.

I am happy I survived, and I am happy we met along the way. I plan to keep on doing this until they shoot me down. I hope you have enjoyed the things I've made up for you. If you didn't, give me another chance. I'm always working on something new, and hopefully better. What can I do? Make-believe is my business.

Carlos Ruiz Zafón

Saints of New York

R.J. Ellory

'Y̲ou're late.'

    'I am.'

'I think you should try and be on time.'

'I did try.'

'Could you try harder?'

'Sure I could.'

'So take a seat, Frank . . . tell me what happened this morning?'

'You can read my report.'

'I want to hear it in your own words.'

'I wrote the report. Those *are* my own words.'

'You know what I mean, Frank. I want to hear you tell me what happened.'

'He cut his girlfriend's throat. He cut his own throat. There was so much fucking blood it was like a water slide at Tomahawk Lake or something. How's that for you?'

'Tell me from the beginning, Frank. From the point you got the call about how he was holding the girl hostage.'

'No.'

'Why not?'

'Because I can't be bothered, that's why. Jesus, what

the fuck *is* this?'

'This is therapeutic counselling, designed to help you deal with the stress of your job and make you feel better. You know that.'

'You want to make me feel better?'

'Sure. That's what I'm here for.'

'Then come over here and take care of me.'

'No, Frank, I am not going to come over there and take care of you.'

'You married?'

'Is that important?'

'Maybe . . . I'm just thinking . . . you got no wedding band, but maybe you just don't wear it 'cause you kinda like burned-out alcoholic cops hitting on you.'

'No, Frank. I don't wear one because I'm not married.'

'Well, how 'bout that! I ain't married neither. So what say I come down here to your cozy little office, we draw the blinds . . . you know how it is. That's the kinda stress counselling I could really use right now.'

'Is that what you feel?'

'Damn right it's what I feel. And I bet you do too, *Doctor*. If only it wasn't for professional ethics, eh?'

'Whatever you say, Frank.'

'Now we're talking.'

'No, Frank, I don't think we're talking at all. You're trying to offend me, and I'm humoring you.'

'Is that what you think I'm doing? Saying shit that will

offend you?'

'I do think that. You're trying to shock me. That stuff about coming over to take care of you, for example.'

'No, Ma'm, that's how I go about courting someone.'

'Well, if that's true, then I figure we're all pretty much safe from the charms of Frank Parrish.'

'That's funny. Now you're trying to make me laugh.'

'No, I'm not. But I *am* trying to give you an opportunity to release some of the stress and trauma that goes with your particular line of work.'

'Oh, shee-it. Save it for the rookies and the faggots and the female officers.'

'That's a very slanted viewpoint.'

'Hey, lady, it's a very fucking slanted world.'

'So you don't want to talk about Tommy Scott and Heather Wallace.'

'That a question or a statement?'

'Whichever.'

'No, I don't want to talk about Tommy Scott and Heather Wallace. What the fuck use would that be?'

'Sometimes people need to talk.'

'Sometimes people need to have other people urinate all over them. Don't mean it does 'em any good.'

'Why do you think you're doing this, Frank?'

'What?'

'Trying to offend me.'

'Lordy, lordy, little girl, you *have* led a sheltered life.

112

You think that's so offensive? Hell, you should hear what I say to members of the general public.'

'I've heard about some of those things.'

'Well, this is me being polite, okay? On my best behavior.'

'Well, your *best behavior* has gotten you eleven verbal cautions, two written warnings, your driver's license suspended, and a one-third pay hold until Christmas. Oh yes – and a recommendation that you see me on a regular basis until your attitude improves.'

'And you think it'll do me some good? Coming on down here and talking to you?'

'I hope so.'

'Why?'

'Because it's what I do, Frank. It's my job, my purpose.'

'And you're a shrink, right?'

'I am a psychotherapist.'

'Psycho-the-rapist.'

'No, Frank, a psychotherapist.'

'I've met a few rapist psychos in my time.'

'I know.'

'You *know*?'

'Yes, Frank, I know some of the people you've had to deal with. I know about some of the things that you've seen.'

'And what does that tell you?'

'It tells me that you're a troubled man. That you might

need someone to talk to.'

'Am I that obvious?'

'Well, yes, I think you are, Frank. I think you are that obvious.'

'You wanna know something we were taught in Keystone Cop School?'

'Sure.'

'Sometimes the obvious occludes the truth. And sometimes things are exactly as they appear.'

'Meaning what?'

'Well, it's real simple. I *appear* to be an aggressive, fucked-up, alcoholic loser with some twenty years on the career clock . . . and you can throw into that incendiary mix my dangerously low self-esteem and a taste for cheap women and expensive whiskey, and you wind up with someone that you really don't want to get involved with. And like I said, even though that is only who I *appear* to be, I think you're gonna find out it's exactly who I am.'

'Well, it looks like we're going to be spending a few really interesting weeks together.'

'You're worried I'm gonna go crazy, aren't you?'

'I don't like to use that term.'

'Oh for God's sake, when did everyone start getting so god-damn scared of words? It's just a *word*, okay? Just a fucking word. Crazy. Crazy. *Crazy*.'

'Okay, so I'm worried that you might go crazy.'

'Some people never go crazy. What truly horrible lives

they must lead.'

'You think that?'

'Bukowski said it. You know Charles Bukowski?'

'He was a drunk, I believe.'

'He was a writer. A writer. Like I am a cop, like you are psycho-the-rapist. The booze doesn't define us lady, it augments the already rich fullness of our lives.'

'You are so full of shit, Frank Parrish.'

'Are you actually allowed to say that to me? Doesn't your professional ethical code prevent you from telling me that I am full of shit?'

'Go home and get some sleep, Frank. Come back and talk to me when you're in a better mood.'

'Hey, that might just be never, Doctor Griffin.'

Somewhere on his desk – somewhere beneath the first officers' reports, the supplementals, the evidence submission slips, the body custody forms, the fingerprint dockets and the interview notes – was a cell phone. It rang now, with a harsh sound, almost bitter, as if accusing Frank Parrish of something.

There were few phone calls that did not have a dead body at the other end. Before the cell phone age those who attended to such matters could have been elsewhere, unreachable. Now the dead bodies found them wherever they were: no hiding and no heroics for the detectives of Homicide Unit Two, Nineteenth Precinct, South Brooklyn. *We get there when the killing's done*, they say. They will also tell you that most murders are brief, brutal and uninteresting. Nine times out of ten they are also pointless.

Like the old saying *Tutte é Mafia in Italia,* everything – just *every*thing – is dead in Homicide.

Parrish located the phone, answered it.

'Frank, it's Hayes here.'

'Hey there. What's up?'

'You know a guy called Danny Lange?'

'Sure I do. Mid-twenties, weaselly-faced kid, did a three-to-five for robbing a drugstore.'

'Yeah. Well, he's dead. Someone put a .22 in his head. You wanna come down here and sort it out?'

Parrish glanced at his watch: it was quarter after five. 'Can do. Where are you?'

Parrish scribbled down the directions, then grabbed one of the uniforms to give him a ride in a squad car. The traffic was bad, jammed up and tight along Adams. They took a right after the Polytechnic University, made better time along Jay, and came out opposite Cathedral Place. Parrish could already see the red flicker from the black-and-whites. They pulled over sharply and Parrish got out, telling the uniform to head on back. To Parrish's left was an empty lot, a derelict coupé hunched like a sad dog, a handful of federal yellow flowers escaping from beneath the hood.

Back of the tapes Danny Lange was spread-eagled on the ground, head at an awkward angle, the expression on his face something akin to mild surprise. He was looking back towards the church at the end of the street. There was a neon sign up there, the light from its tubes subdued by smog and dirt, that Parrish knew well. *Sin Will Find You Out*. No shit, Sherlock, he had thought the first time he saw it.

'You turned him yet?' Parrish asked Paul Hayes.

'Ain't done a thing,' Hayes said.

'No change there then,' Parrish quipped.

'Go fuck yourself, Parrish,' Hayes replied, but he was half-smiling. 'There's a deli half a block down. You want anything?'

'See if you can get me some Vicodin. If not, aspirin. And a cup of coffee. Black and strong.'

Hayes disappeared.

Down on his haunches, Frank Parrish surveyed the body silently for some minutes, aware that darkness was dropping fast. He sensed the uniforms watching him from the black-and-whites.

Danny had leaked, just a little. That was not unusual for such a small caliber. It would be up to the ME to make a call on this as the primary or secondary crime scene. This was the drop, nothing more. Parrish put on latex gloves, went through Danny's pockets, found the better part of a hundred bucks which he tucked discreetly into his shoe. No ID, no driver's license, no billfold, no watch. Still, despite such missing artifacts, this was no robbery. Danny Lange was not a man to wear a watch or carry a billfold, or even a man who washed, for that matter. Dying had not tempered his characteristically rank odor.

The hole in his throat was the only wound. Entry, no exit. Looked like the .22 had actually been pointed upwards at a steep angle, leaving the bullet still inside his head. Those little slugs had insufficient power to make it a through-and-through; they would just ricochet around like a fairground ride and mush the brain. Number of times they collided with the internal wall of the cranium just pancaked the shit out of them. Difficult to pull any lands, grooves, striations. Parrish used his little finger to push up into the entry wound. It was still moist an inch or so in, telling him Danny had been dead no more than a couple of hours. Danny Lange was small time. No money, no future, little of anything at all. He would have pissed someone off, short-changed them, cut a deal with something obvious like baby laxative or baking soda, and that was that. It was all the same, and it was all war. Parrish knew his Cormac McCarthy. The old judge in *Blood Meridian* said, "It makes no difference what men think of war. War endures. As well ask men what they think of stone. War was always here. Before Man was, war waited for him . . . That is the way it was and will be."

The war had reached Danny Lange, and he was now one of its countless casualties.

Frank Parrish called one of the uniforms over, gave him some gloves, told him to help him roll the vic. They did. Danny had crapped himself.

'You call the DC?' Frank asked.

'Yes, sir, I did.'

'Good man. You wait here and keep an eye on him. Make sure he don't do a runner. I'm gonna go drink some coffee with my friend, and I'll speak to the deputy coroner when he comes down, okay?'

'Yes, sir.'

Hayes had made it as far as Starbucks. No Vicodin, only aspirin, but at least the coffee was passable. Parrish chewed a couple of tablets and washed them down.

'Anything?' Hayes asked.

Parrish shook his head. 'Usual shit. He must've upset someone. Someone said something. Like the Sicilians say, a word in the right ear can make or murder a man.'

'How many you got on?'

'Three,' Parrish replied.

'I already got five open. Can you take this one?'

Parrish hesitated.

'You take this one and I'll give you a credit on my next bust.'

Parrish nodded. 'Deal.'

'You got your partner yet?' Hayes asked.

'Tomorrow,' Parrish said. 'Some nineteen-year-old out of detective school.'

'Hope that works out for you.'

'Me I ain't worried about. It's whatever dumb schmuck they give me'll have the problem. He better be able to look round corners.'

'So, we're good? I'm away. Leave you to deal with the DC.'

Hayes walked back two steps, turned and disappeared. Parrish heard his car start around the corner and pull away sharply.

He drank half the coffee, tipped the rest into the road, dropped the cup into a basket at the corner, and walked back to Danny Lange.

The Deputy Coroner came and went. Parrish watched the wagon take Danny away, and then walked to the nearest subway station.

Danny Lange's place was a flea-bitten rat-hole of a shithouse up on the ninth floor of some project building. Even as Parrish approached the entrance, he remembered an earlier time he'd been there. Two years ago, maybe three. He'd come away feeling the need to wash his hair and dry-clean his clothes. It was a sad day when a man lost his reason, sadder when he lost his respect. Danny Lange had lost both a long time ago.

The inner hallway smelled of piss and puke. A scattering of used hypodermics crunched underfoot as Parrish skirted the elevators and headed for the stairwell. The elevators were notoriously unreliable, the very worst kind of place to get trapped.

He reached the third and was already out of breath. He was alone. Shouldn't have been, but partners wore out quicker than they used to – last one took a permanent rain check. Parrish had done his first three years as a detective in Vice, the next six in Robbery-Homicide, and when they split the units he stayed with the dead people. Robbery was bullshit. Penny-ante liquor store hold-ups, some Korean guy dead for the sake of twenty-nine dollars and change. Junkies working for enough money to score pep-pills, trying to stave off the heebie-jeebies. Heebie-jeebies gonna getcha no matter how many stores you rob. That was just the way of things.

Fifth floor and Parrish took a break. He would have smoked a cigarette but he couldn't breathe. He stopped, tried not to think of Caitlin, his daughter, but she came at him every which way. *Get more exercise, Dad. Smoke less cigarettes. And don't even get me started on the drinking.*

He wasn't winning. She was almost done with her training, and he wanted her close – Brooklyn Hospital, Cumberland, even Holy Family down on Dean Street, but Caitlin wanted to go to Manhattan. St. Vincent's perhaps. She had gone for nursing; something her mother had always supported. And Caitlin's mother was Frank's ex-wife. Clare Parrish. Except now she'd reverted to her maiden name of Baxter. Fuck it. How did that ever go so wrong? Sure, they were married young, but it had been good. December '85 they'd gotten hitched. Robert was born just four months later in April of '86, Caitlin in June of '88. Good kids. Better than their parents. Such a great start. Difficulties, yes of course, but nothing major, nothing serious. How that deteriorated into a barrage of vitriolic accusations – unfounded for the most part – he would never know. Silent grievances saved up like bad pennies. He was aggressive, bull-headed, ignorant, forgetful. She was shallow, cynical, untrusting, dismissive of his friends. Friends . . . What friends?

And then it turned really bitter. He failed to understand *even the most rudimentary requirements for social interaction*. She *could not cook, clean,* she had *no culture, no passion*. Afterwards, the argument spent, they would get drunk and fuck like rampant teenagers, but it was never the same and they both knew it. Each had uttered sharp words, and between them – neither more guilty than the other – they had pricked the matrimonial bubble. Tolerance deflated. He had rented a three-room apartment on South Portland, started an affair with a twenty-seven-year-old paralegal named Holly. Clare started screwing her hairstylist – half-Italian with a ponytail – who called her *bambino* and left fingernail crescents on her ass.

Hindsight, ever and again the cruelest and most astute advisor, gave him harsh lessons in responsibility. He should have had a better attitude. He should have appreciated that his wife – despite the fact that she did not work in Homicide – nevertheless had an important job raising a family. All well and good now, after it had blown itself skywards. *Most guys*, she used to say, *you have to wait for them to fuck up. You? With you there ain't no waiting. You're a fuck-up before you arrive.*

Divorce had gone through in November 2001, when Caitlin was thirteen, Robert two years older. Clare got them weekdays, Frank had them weekends. They got their diplomas, went to college, started to take their own bold steps in the world. They were undoubtedly the best thing that came out of it. They were the very best part of him.

Parrish reached the ninth and was ready to fold. He stayed for a while, leaning against the wall, heart thudding. A black woman opened the door of one of the apartments, looked him up and down like he'd gotten his dick out and shook it at her. She asked nothing, said nothing, closed the door again.

He tried a deep breath, headed down the hallway, and let himself into Danny Lange's apartment with the key he'd taken from Danny's pocket. Everything else he'd signed over to Evidence Control and left for Crime Scene to pick up.

The lights were on, and the place smelled ripe.

She wasn't yet old enough to show any wear on her face, not even in her eyes – eyes that looked back at him with the quiet and hopeful surprise so evident in all unexpected deaths. She was naked but for her underwear, her skin the color of alabaster; white, with that faint shadow of blue that comes a little while after the breathing stops. The thing that really surprised Frank Parrish was that he was not surprised at all. A dead girl on Danny Lange's bed. Just like that. Later, he even remembered he'd said something to her, though he could not recall what it was.

He pulled up a chair and sat for a while in silence. He guessed she was sixteen, perhaps seventeen. These days it was so hard to tell. Her hair was cut shoulder length and hung down around her face. She was beautiful, no question, and the care and precision with which she had applied red polish to her fingernails and toenails was something to behold. She was almost perfect in every sense, save for the livid bruising around the base of her throat. Confirmation of strangulation came when Parrish knelt on the floor and looked directly into her eyes with his flashlight. The tiny red spots of petechial hemorrhaging were there – present on her eyelids, and also behind her ears.

He had not seen Danny Lange for a couple of years.

Then, the guy had been a junkie and a thief, not a killer. But hell, times had changed. It wasn't that people did worse things than they had fifteen or twenty years before, it was simply that more people did them.

Parrish called it in. Dispatch said they'd inform the Coroner's Office and Crime Scene Unit. Parrish went around the apartment – the front room, the kitchen, the narrow bathroom, then back to the girl on the bed. There was something strangely familiar about her, and then he realized what it was. She looked like Danny.

Fifteen minutes later Parrish's suspicions were confirmed. He found a small bundle of pictures – Mom, Danny, the dead girl on the bed. A hundred-to-one she was Danny's baby sister. In the pictures she was no more than ten or eleven, bright like a firework, all smiles and freckles. Danny looked real, like he had yet to hit the dope. Mom and the two kids – a regular snapshot from the family album. Was there such a thing as a regular family, or did shadows lurk behind the front door of every home?

He pulled a clip-top evidence bag from his jacket pocket and dropped the photos into it. Then he went and sat back in the chair near the bed. He wanted to stay with the girl until everyone else arrived.

An hour and a half later Parrish was in a window booth in a diner on Joralemon Street near St. Francis College, a plate of food in front of him. He'd managed just a few mouthfuls, but that acid burning was back, somewhere low in the base of his gut. An ulcer perhaps. If he saw a doctor he would be told it was the booze. *Cut back on the booze*, the guy would say. *Man your age should remember that the body hurts faster, heals slower.*

Parrish perused the half-dozen pages of notes he'd taken in Danny Lange's place. There was nothing much of anything. Deputy Coroner had shipped the girl out, tied and tagged, and she would be autopsied tonight or, more likely, tomorrow. Coroner's initial findings at the scene accorded with his own.

'Thumb prints here and here,' he told Parrish. 'Fingers here and here and here. Marks are darker on the left side of her neck, which means whoever choked her was more than likely a rightie. You can't be absolute on that, but it's a strong possibility.'

The DC had checked beneath her fingernails for skin, combed her hair and her pubes for foreigns, checked inside her mouth, looked for cuts, bruises, abrasions, bite marks, needle punctures, indications of tape adhesive on the ankles and wrists, rope-burns, signs of restraint, subcutaneous hemorrhaging, external residues of toxic elements, semen, saliva and blood. She was pretty clean.

'I can do a rape kit, confirm COD, and get word back to you within twenty-four, maybe forty-eight hours,' the DC had said. 'Might be able to get a tox done, but that'll take a little longer. At a guess, she's been dead . . . I dunno . . . about eight hours, I'd say. Laking indicates that this is the primary. I don't think she was moved.'

They pressed latex and Parrish left.

So Parrish went to a diner and had tuna casserole, a bagel, some coffee. The casserole was good but the appetite was gone. He kept thinking back to Eve, to the fact that he couldn't get it up that morning. Seemed he was losing everything by inches. He was on the way out. He needed to take some exercise, cut back on the smokes, the drinks, the hydrogenated fats, the carbs, the shakes and chips and Oreos. He needed a vacation, but he knew he wouldn't take one.

His father used to say something: *What do you want most? And what would you do to get it?*

To this he could now add his own variation: *What do you fear most? And what would you do to avoid it?*

Right now, what he most wanted to avoid was another session with the psychotherapist.

Why I wrote . . .

Saints of New York

In early 2009, just two days after Obama was inaugurated, I arrived in Washington DC with a BBC film crew. We were there to make a documentary piece about my book, *A Simple Act of Violence*. I spent a day with the FBI, another day at the offices of the *Washington Post*, but there was one interview that stood head and shoulders above the rest.

We drove up into Fallschurch, Virginia, and here I met June Boyle, a thirteen-year veteran homicide detective. June was immediately charming, and on benches near a snow-covered playground she spoke of her life in the Fairfax County Police Department.

June was the lead police investigator in the Washington Sniper case, the most important investigation on the east coast for as many years as anyone could remember. June was the detective who secured a confession from Lee Boyd Malvo, the younger of the two assassins. She spent six and a half hours with him. She gained his confidence and his trust. She arranged his food; she sent out for veggie burgers, for boxes of raisins. She got him to open up, to really start talking, and with that information the case had a foundation and a grounding that could never have been possible without her.

Despite the fact that the US Attorney General authorised Malvo's trial to take place in Virginia, thus giving the jury the opportunity to invoke the death penalty, they in fact gave him life in prison. Asked about this, June's expression changed completely. 'Malvo should be dead,' she replied, so coldly, so matter-of-factly. 'There are some people in this world that should be dead, and Malvo is one of them.' It was a glimpse behind the face she wore for the world. In that moment I realised that despite her generosity of spirit, she was first and foremost a police detective, and had been witness to some of the very worst kind of people the world had to offer. This was a lifestyle, a vocation that one could never leave behind. She, of all the people I met, gave me the greatest insight into the minds of characters I chose to write about.

Towards the end of the interview I asked her to summarise her life as a homicide investigator. She smiled wryly, and then she produced two mobile phones. She held them out, one in each hand. 'This one is my personal phone,' she said, 'and it never rings. Whereas this one is for work, and it rings all the time.' That simple demonstration seemed to say everything.

'I take a call,' she went on. 'And there's always a dead body at the other end. My day starts when their day ends. And I go out to that murder scene, and there's some twelve-year-old girl in a dumpster, or it's a hit and run or a domestic, and while I'm there the phone rings again, and someone else's life is over. After a while that's gonna get right inside you.'

Then we talked about missing persons. We spoke of the 850,000 Missing Persons Reports filed every year. We spoke of the vast majority of reports that were resolved, and the small percentage that were not. The forgotten victims.

And it was that conversation that gave birth to the idea of Frank Parrish and *Saints of New York*. The forgotten victims. The ones that were never found. A single man's obsession to find the truth of what had really happened to a girl. A girl that no-one even missed.

Frank Parrish, the lead character in *Saints*, is asked by a colleague. 'Why, Frank . . . why are you so determined to find out what happened to this girl? For Christ's sake . . . no-one else even cares.'

'That's why,' Parrish replies. 'Precisely because no-one else does.'

Saints, however, is not about police procedure. It is not about the kidnapping of teenagers and their exploitation in the sex industry. It is not about the way in which this

130

job is done.

It deals with these subjects, of course, but really it is about the men and women who do that job, about one man specifically, about the effect that such a job has on his life.

It is about how far one man will go to find justice for those who've been forgotten by the rest of the world.

R. J. Ellory

The Passage

Justin Cronin

Before she became the Girl from Nowhere – the One Who Walked In, the First and Last and Only, who lived a thousand years – she was just a little girl in Iowa, named Amy. Amy Harper Bellafonte.

The day Amy was born, her mother, Jeanette, was nineteen years old. Jeanette named her baby Amy for her own mother, who'd died when Jeanette was little, and gave her the middle name Harper for Harper Lee, the lady who'd written *To Kill a Mockingbird,* Jeanette's favorite book – truth be told, the only book she'd made it all the way through in high school. She might have named her Scout, after the little girl in the story, because she wanted her little girl to grow up like that, tough and funny and wise, in a way that she, Jeanette, had never managed to be. But Scout was a name for a boy, and she didn't want her daughter to have to go around her whole life explaining something like that.

Amy's father was a man who came in one day to the restaurant where Jeanette had waited tables since she turned sixteen, a diner everyone called the Box, because it looked like one: like a big chrome shoe box sitting off the county road, backed by fields of corn and beans, nothing else around for miles except a self-serve car wash, the kind where you had to put coins into the machine and do all the work yourself. The man, whose name was Bill Reynolds, sold combines and harvesters, big things like that, and he was a sweet talker who told Jeanette as she poured his coffee and then later, again and again, how pretty she was, how he liked her coal-black hair and hazel eyes and slender wrists, said it all in a way that sounded like he meant it, not the way boys in school had, as if the words were just something that needed to get said along the way to her letting them do as they liked. He had a big car, a new Pontiac, with a dashboard that glowed like a spaceship and leather seats creamy as butter. She could have loved that man, she thought, really and truly loved him. But he stayed in town only a few days, and then went on his way. When she told her father what had happened, he said he wanted to go looking for him, make him live up to his responsibilities. But what Jeanette knew and didn't say was that Bill Reynolds was married, a married man; he had a family in Lincoln, all the way clean over in Nebraska. He'd even showed her the pictures in his wallet of his kids, two little boys in baseball uniforms, Bobby and Billy. So no matter how many times her father asked who the man was that had done this to her, she didn't say. She didn't even tell him the man's name.

And the truth was, she didn't mind any of it, not really:

not the being pregnant, which was easy right until the end, nor the delivery itself, which was bad but fast, nor, especially, having a baby, her little Amy. To tell Jeanette he'd decided to forgive her, her father had done up her brother's old bedroom as a nursery, carried down the old baby crib from the attic, the one Jeanette herself had slept in, years ago; he'd gone with Jeanette, in the last months before Amy came, to the Walmart to pick out some things she'd need, like pajamas and a little plastic tub and a wind-up mobile to hang over the crib. He'd read a book that said that babies needed things like that, things to look at so their little brains would turn on and begin to work properly. From the start Jeanette always thought of the baby as 'her,' because in her heart she wanted a girl, but she knew that wasn't the sort of thing you should say to anyone, not even to yourself. She'd had a scan at the hospital over in Cedar Falls and asked the woman, a lady in a flowered smock who was running the little plastic paddle over Jeanette's stomach, if she could tell which it was; but the woman laughed, looking at the pictures on the TV of Jeanette's baby, sleeping away inside her, and said, *Hon, this baby's shy. Sometimes you can tell and others you can't, and this is one of those times.* So Jeanette didn't know, which she decided was fine with her, and after she and her father had emptied out her brother's room and taken down his old pennants and posters – Jose Canseco, a music group called Killer Picnic, the Bud Girls – and seen how faded and banged up the walls were, they painted it a color the label on the can called 'Dreamtime,' which somehow was both pink and blue at once – good whatever the baby turned out to be. Her father hung a wallpaper border along the edge of the ceiling, a repeating pattern of ducks splashing in a puddle, and cleaned up an old maple rocking chair he'd found at the auction hall, so that when Jeanette brought the baby home, she'd have a place to sit and hold her.

The baby came in summer, the girl she'd wanted and named Amy Harper Bellafonte; there seemed no point in using the name Reynolds, the last name of a man Jeanette guessed she'd never see again and, now that Amy was here, no longer wanted to. And Bellafonte: you couldn't do better than a name like that. It meant 'beautiful fountain,' and that's what Amy was. Jeanette fed and rocked and changed her, and when Amy cried in the middle of the night because she was wet or hungry or didn't like the dark, Jeanette stumbled down the hall to her room, no matter what the hour was or how tired she felt from working at the Box, to pick her up and tell her she was there, she would always be there, you cry and I'll come running, that's a deal between us, you and me, forever and ever, my little Amy Harper Bellafonte. And she would hold and rock her until dawn began to pale the window shades and she could hear birds singing in the branches of the trees outside.

Then Amy was three and Jeanette was alone. Her

father had died, a heart attack they told her, or else a stroke. It wasn't the kind of thing anyone needed to check. Whatever it was, it hit him early one winter morning as he was walking to his truck to drive to work at the elevator; he had just enough time to put down his coffee on the fender before he fell over and died, never spilling a drop. She still had her job at the Box, but the money wasn't enough now, not for Amy or any of it, and her brother, in the Navy somewhere, didn't answer her letters. *God invented Iowa,* he always said, *so people could leave it and never come back*. She wondered what she would do.

Then one day a man came into the diner. It was Bill Reynolds. He was different, somehow, and the change was no good. The Bill Reynolds she remembered – and she had to admit she still thought of him from time to time, about little things mostly, like the way his sandy hair flopped over his forehead when he talked, or how he blew over his coffee before he sipped it, even when it wasn't hot anymore – there was something about him, a kind of warm light from inside that you wanted to be near. It reminded her of those little plastic sticks that you snapped so the liquid inside made them glow. This was the same man, but the glow was gone. He looked older, thinner. She saw he hadn't shaved or combed his hair, which was greasy and standing all which-away, and he wasn't wearing a pressed polo like before but just an ordinary work shirt like the ones her father had worn, untucked and stained under the arms. He looked like he'd spent all night out in the weather, or in a car somewhere. He caught her eye at the door and she followed him to a booth in the back.

—*What are you doing here?*

—*I left her,* he said, and as he looked at where she stood, she smelled beer on his breath, and sweat, and dirty clothes. *I've gone and done it, Jeanette. I left my wife. I'm a free man.*

—*You drove all this way to tell me that?*

—*I've thought about you.* He cleared his throat. *A lot. I've thought about us.*

—*What us? There ain't no us. You can't come in like you're doing and say you've been thinking about us.*

He sat up straight. —*Well, I'm doing it. I'm doing it right now.*

—It's busy in here, can't you see that? I can't be talking to you like this. You'll have to order something.

—Fine, he answered, but he didn't look at the menu on the wall, just kept his eyes on her. *I'll have a cheeseburger. A cheeseburger and a Coke.*

As she wrote down the order and the words swam in her vision, she realized she had started to cry. She felt like she hadn't slept in a month, a year. The weight of exhaustion was held up only by the thinnest sliver of her will. There was a time when she'd wanted to do something with her life – cut hair, maybe, get her certificate, open a little shop, move to a real city, like Chicago or Des Moines, rent an apartment, have friends. She'd always held in her mind a picture of herself sitting in a restaurant, a coffee shop but nice; it was fall, and cold outside, and she was alone at a small table by the window, reading a book. On her table was a steaming mug of tea. She would look up to the window to see the people on the street of the city she was in, hustling to and fro in their heavy coats and hats, and see her own face there, too, reflected in the window, hovering over the image of all the people outside. But as she stood there, these ideas seemed like they belonged to a different person entirely. Now there was Amy, sick half the time with a cold or a stomach thing she'd gotten at the ratty day care where she spent the days while Jeanette was working at the Box, and her father dead just like that, so fast it was as if he'd fallen through a trapdoor on the surface of the earth, and Bill Reynolds sitting at the table like he'd just stepped out for a second, not four years.

—*Why are you doing this to me?*

He held her eyes with his own a long moment and touched the top of her hand. —*Meet me later. Please.*

He ended up living in the house with her and Amy. She couldn't say if she had invited him to do this or if it had just somehow happened. Either way, she was instantly sorry. This Bill Reynolds: who was he really? He'd left his wife and boys, Bobby and Billy in their baseball suits, all of it behind in Nebraska. The Pontiac was gone, and he had no job either; that had ended, too. The economy the way it was, he explained, nobody was buying a goddamn thing. He said he had a plan, but the only plan that she could see seemed to be him sitting in the house doing nothing for Amy or even cleaning up the breakfast dishes, while she worked all day at the Box. He hit her the first time after he'd been living there three months; he was drunk, and once he did it, he burst out crying and said, over and over, how sorry he was. He was on his knees, blubbering, like *she'd* done something to *him*. She had to understand, he was saying, how hard it all was, all the changes in his life, it was more than a man, any man, could take. He loved her, he was sorry, nothing like that would happen again, ever. He *swore* it. Not to her and not to Amy. And in the end, she heard herself saying she was sorry too.

He'd hit her over money; when winter came, and she didn't have enough money in her checking account to pay the heating oil man, he hit her again.

—*Goddamnit, woman. Can't you see I'm in a situation here?*

She was on the kitchen floor, holding the side of her head. He'd hit her hard enough to lift her off her feet. Funny, now that she was down there she saw how dirty the floor was, filthy and stained, with clumps of dust and who-knew-what all rowed against the base of the cabinets where you couldn't usually see. Half her mind was noticing this while the other half said, You aren't thinking straight, Jeanette; Bill hit you and knocked a wire loose, so now you're worrying over the dust. Something funny was happening with the way the world sounded, too. Amy was watching television upstairs, on the little set in her room, but Jeanette could hear it like it was playing inside her head, Barney the purple dinosaur and a song about brushing your teeth; and then from far away, she heard the sound of the oil truck pulling away, its engine grinding as it turned out of the drive and headed down the county road.

—*It ain't your house,* she said.

—*You're right about that.* Bill took a bottle of Old Crow from over the sink and poured some in a jelly jar, though it was only ten o'clock in the morning. He sat at the table but didn't cross his legs like he meant to get comfortable. *Ain't my oil, either.*

Jeanette rolled over and tried to stand but couldn't. She watched him drink for a minute.

—*Get out.*

He laughed, shaking his head, and took a sip of whiskey.

—*That's funny,* he said. *You telling me that from the floor like you are.*

—*I mean what I say. Get out.*

Amy came into the room. She was holding the stuffed bunny she still carried everywhere, and wearing a pair of overalls, the good ones Jeanette had bought her at the outlet mall, the OshKosh B'Gosh, with the strawberries embroidered on the bib. One of the straps had come undone and was flopping at her waist. Jeanette realized Amy must have done this herself, because she had to go to the bathroom.

—*You're on the floor, Mama.*

—*I'm okay, honey.* She got to her feet to show her. Her left ear was ringing a little, like in a cartoon, birds flying around her head. She saw there was a little blood, too, on her hand; she didn't know where this had come from. She picked Amy up and did her best to smile. *See? Mama just took a spill, that's all. You need to go, honey? You need to use the potty?*

—*Look at you,* Bill was saying. *Will you look at yourself?* He shook his head again and drank. *You stupid twat. She probably ain't even mine.*

—*Mama,* the girl said and pointed, *you cut yourself. Your nose is cut.*

And whether it was what she'd heard or the blood, the little girl began to cry.

—*See what you done?* Bill said, and to Amy, *Come on now. Ain't no big thing, sometimes folks argue, that's just how it is.*

—*I'm telling you again, just leave.*

—*Then what would you do, tell me that. You can't even fill the oil tank.*

—*You think I don't know that? I sure as by God don't need you to tell me that.*

Amy had begun to wail. Holding her, Jeanette felt the spread of hot moisture across her waist as the little girl released her bladder.

—*For Pete's sake, shut that kid up.*

She held Amy tight against her chest. —*You're right. She ain't yours. She ain't yours and never will be. You leave or I'm calling the sheriff, I swear.*

—*Don't you do me like this, Jean. I mean it.*

—*Well, I'm doing it. That's just what I'm doing.*

Then he was up and slamming through the house, taking his things, tossing them back into the cardboard cartons he'd used to carry them into the house, months ago. Why hadn't she thought it right then, how strange it was that he didn't even have a proper suitcase? She sat at the kitchen table holding Amy on her lap, watching the clock over the stove and counting off the minutes until he returned to the kitchen to hit her again.

But then she heard the front door swing open, and his heavy footsteps on the porch. He went in and out awhile, carrying the boxes, leaving the front door open so cold air spilled through the house. Finally he came into the kitchen, tracking snow, leaving little patches of it waffled to the floor with the soles of his boots.

—*Fine. Fine. You want me to leave? You watch me.* He took the bottle of Old Crow from the table. *Last chance,* he said.

Jeanette said nothing, didn't even look at him.

—So that's how it is. Fine. You mind I have one for the road?

Which was when Jeanette reached out and swatted his glass across the kitchen, smacked it with her open hand like a ping-pong ball with a paddle. She knew she was going to do this for about half a second before she did, knowing it wasn't the best idea she'd ever had, but by then it was too late. The glass hit the wall with a hollow thud and fell to the floor, unbroken. She closed her eyes, holding Amy tight, knowing what would come. For a moment the sound of the glass rolling on the floor seemed to be the only thing in the room. She could feel Bill's anger rising off him like waves of heat.

—You just see what the world has in store for you, Jeanette. You remember I said that.

Then his footsteps carried him out of the room and he was gone.

She paid the oil man what she could and turned the thermostat down to fifty, to make it last. *See, Amy honey, it's like a big camping trip we're on,* she said as she stuffed the little girl's hands into mittens and wedged a hat onto her head. *There now, it's not so cold, not really. It's like an adventure.* They slept together under a pile of old quilts, the room so icy their breath fogged the air over their faces. She took a job at night, cleaning up at the high school, leaving Amy with a neighbor lady, but when the woman took sick and had to go into the hospital, Jeanette had to leave Amy alone. She explained to Amy what to do: stay in bed, don't answer the door, just close your eyes and I'll be home before you know it. She'd make sure Amy was asleep before creeping out the door, then stride quickly down the snow-crusted drive to where she'd parked her car, away from the house, so Amy wouldn't hear it turning over.

But then she made the mistake one night of telling someone about this, another woman on the work crew, when the two of them had stepped out for a smoke. Jeanette had never liked smoking at all and didn't want to spend the money, but the cigarettes helped her stay awake, and without a smoke break there was nothing to look forward to, just more toilets to scrub and halls to be mopped. She told the woman, whose name was Alice, not to tell anyone, she knew she could get in trouble leaving Amy alone like that, but of course that's just what Alice did; she went straight to the superintendent, who fired Jeanette on the spot. *Leaving a child like that ain't right,* he told her in his office by the boilers, a room no bigger than ten feet square with a dented metal desk and an old easy chair with the plush popping out and a calendar on the wall that wasn't even the right year; the air was always so hot and close in there Jeanette could barely breathe. He said, *You count your lucky stars I'm not calling the county on you.* She wondered when she'd become someone a person could say this to and not be wrong. He'd been nice enough to her until then, and maybe she could have made him understand the situation, that without the money from cleaning she didn't know what she'd do, but she was too tired to find the words. She took her last check and drove home in her crappy old car, the Kia she'd bought in high school when it was already six years old and falling apart so fast she could practically see the nuts and bolts bouncing on the pavement in her rearview mirror; and when she stopped at the Quick Mart to buy a pack of Capris and then the engine wouldn't start up again, she started to cry. She couldn't make herself stop crying for half an hour.

The problem was the battery; a new one cost her eighty-three dollars at Sears, but by then she'd missed a week of work and lost her job at the Box, too. She had just enough money left to leave, packing up their things in a couple of grocery sacks and the cartons Bill had left behind.

Why I wrote . . .

The Passage

You write the book that asks to be written, and *The Passage* asked me to write it on a series of long jogs in the fall of 2005, taken in the company of my daughter, Iris, age eight, who rode beside me on her bicycle. For many years, running has been part of my writing ritual. I do my best creative thinking while running, which I have come to understand as a form of self-hypnosis. It's here I get my ideas, but not just my ideas; on the best days, whole paragraphs seem to drop into my head.

Iris is the reader every writer longs for – when she loves a book, she loves it unreservedly – but she is also the critic we all fear, capable of skewering a novel she doesn't like with the most withering sarcasm. That day as we set out, our conversation naturally turned to books and writing, and Iris made a confession: your books, daddy, are boring. She said this offhandedly, as if she were telling me something I probably already knew. I might have been offended but I was mostly surprised; I didn't know she'd read them. But when I asked her about this, she said she hadn't read them, not exactly; she knew my books were boring, she explained, from their covers, and the summaries on the flaps. Well, that's literary novels, I explained, relieved. Sometimes it's hard to say exactly what they're about, in so many words. To which my daughter rolled her eyes. That's what I mean, said Iris. Boring. 'Well what do you want me to write about?' I asked. She took a moment to think. 'A girl who saves the world,' she said. I had to laugh. It was a classic dare, and I knew it. 'OK,' I said. 'Let's do it together. We can toss ideas around, see if we can work it into a story.' She agreed, and across that fall to pass the time of our afternoon run-rides, we began to formulate the plot of a novel, and gradually the story and its details came into shape. Despite what I had said, I had no intention of actually writing the thing, writing and talking being in the end two entirely different matters, one much more work than the other.

And then a funny thing happened. As the weeks went by, I began to think this story actually could be a book, and that it was actually a better book than the one I was actually supposed to be writing.

For three months, Iris and I traded ideas back and forth; by December, we had the plot worked out, right down to the final scene. I felt sad, as if something wonderful was ending, and I decided not to let it end; I sat at my computer and began to write an outline, so I wouldn't forget it. And when that was done, I decided I would write the first chapter. Just to see how it felt.

Justin Cronin